The Tears of Poseidon

Other Books by Debbie Viguié

The Psalm 23 Mysteries

The Lord is My Shepherd
I Shall Not Want
Lie Down in Green Pastures
Beside Still Waters
Restoreth My Soul
In the Paths of Righteousness
For His Name's Sake
Walk Through the Valley
The Shadow of Death

The Kiss Trilogy

Kiss of Night
Kiss of Death
Kiss of Revenge

Witch Hunt series

The Thirteenth Sacrifice
The Last Grave
Circle of Blood

Other Books by Dr. Scott C. Viguié

Archaeology in Fiction

The Tears of Poseidon

A Tex Ravencroft Adventure

Debbie Viguié

and

Dr. Scott C. Viguié

Cover Art by Matt Washburn

Published by Eureka Publications

The Tears of Poseidon

ISBN-13: 978-0692275306

Published by Eureka Publications

www.eurekapublications.com

To Rita De La Torre for her friendship and support.

-DV

To Jason De La Torre, a fellow Atlantis enthusiast.

-SV

ACKNOWLEDGEMENTS

Thank you to the love of my life (who just happens to be my coauthor for this book). I love the world we've created together and I can't wait to see what Tex does next.

Thank you to everyone who helped make this book a reality, particularly Rick and Barbara Reynolds. Thank you to Matt Washburn for his fantastic cover art. I also need to say thank you to family and friends who were patient with us while we had our heads down and were hard at work.

-DV

I would like to thank my soul mate, wife and co-author Debbie Viguié for agreeing to help me translate Tex's adventures from a few diary entries to his own adventures.

Likewise, I would like to thank Rick and Barbara Reynolds for their support and insight as we meshed two very different styles

-SV

AUTHORS' NOTE

The adventures of archaeologist Charles "Tex" Ravencroft, in the form of diary entries, were originally conceived as fictional illustrations for the book *Archaeology in Fiction.* The book was written to compare and contrast archaeology as seen in movies and television with real archaeology. It was based on a series of lectures given by Dr. Scott C. Viguié. In *Archaeology in Fiction* every chapter begins with an excerpt from Tex's journals.

Creating this character was a wonderful experience and together with his wife, Debbie, Scott decided to flesh out the stories about Tex. This book is the first in a trilogy encompassing the adventure that Tex had which was hinted at in *Archaeology in Fiction.* Readers who want to know more about how fictional archaeology matches up to real archaeology or those who want a sneak peek at what's coming later in this series should read *Archaeology in Fiction.*

Chapter 1

June 9, 1931

Tex Ravencroft knew there was every chance he was about to die. He had faced death before, but this time it felt closer to him, like an itch on the back of his neck as though some unseen being was breathing on him. A step on his trail, that's what the old timers would say. Maybe they were right.

"What is wrong?" his local guide, Kai, asked.

"Probably nothing," Tex said, incapable of offering more reassurance than that. The truth was, they were already in six different kinds of trouble. They were trespassing on grounds sacred to the Hawaiian people. The coconut groves on the east coast of Kauai were *kapu*, forbidden, at least to commoners. They were meant for royalty alone.

Tex Ravencroft was a lot of things, a teacher, an explorer, an archaeologist, to name a few, but royalty he most certainly was not. Not for the first time he wondered if he needed to seriously reconsider his career choices.

Still, the monarchy was over, Hawaii was a territory of the United States. No royals were claiming the land, defending it against invaders such as him. At least, that was the theory. He still couldn't shake the feeling, though, that he was in danger.

The air was moist and fragrant, pressing against him like a living, tangible thing as he made his way through the trees, stepping over fallen coconuts. He had come here chasing a legend, the way he so often did. For years he had collected several obscure references to a carved stone goblet. The ancient Hawaiians had used it in their human sacrifice rituals. The goblet was supposedly possessed of the power to destroy a man's soul if used in a certain way.

Personally, he didn't go in for that kind of thing. The world was a strange enough place without adding in mystical, supernatural elements. The rarity of the goblet, though, and its place in legend were enough of an enticement to bring him here in search of it. Treasures like this were meant to be shared with the world. And, if the museum happened to pay him to acquire objects like this, well, even an archaeologist needed to put food on the table.

He glanced behind him. The slim trunks of the coconut trees were all that was there. There was no vast army of warriors waiting even though it felt like there was. He turned back and as he did a glimmer of light caught his eye. It looked like light reflecting off the water.

The ocean was behind them, so this was something different. He felt his spirits lift slightly. He was looking for a pond and maybe this was it. He angled off in that direction and about fifty feet later it came into view. The pond itself was narrow, but very long so that from where he was standing on the one bank he couldn't quite see the other one. The roughly rectangular shape was unusual, and he couldn't tell if it was natural or shaped by the hand of man.

Partway down the left side he spotted a small section of lava rock wall lining the pond. The regularity of the lines betrayed it as man-made. He moved toward it with Kai trailing behind.

"So many things are changing," Kai said. "More and more of your kind are coming here. Others, too. Puerto Ricans come to work the sugar plantations. Many from Korea, also. Soon our children will lose much of their memory of the old times and nothing will be sacred anymore."

"If you don't want to be here in the royal coconut groves then why did you bring me?" Tex asked.

"Someone was going to bring you, and I might as well have the money for it. Things are changing quickly, too quickly, but a man is wise to look to his future even if he does mourn his past."

"And what is that future looking like?" Tex asked while keeping his eyes fixed on the lava wall.

"My eyes are telling me that this would be a wonderful location for a hotel."

Tex barely managed to hold back a laugh. "Tell you what. You build it and I'll be your first guest."

"It is agreed then," Kai said.

Tex stopped as he reached the edge of the lava rock wall. There was a recessed ledge cut into it on the side facing the pond. The ledge held two objects. The first, a skull, bore a grotesque looking grin as though it was mocking all who came before it. It was not the first mocking skull Tex had come across in his travels, and they all served a single purpose. They were a warning to those who would dare continue in their search.

The second item on the ledge was a white ceramic cat brightly painted with a single paw raised.

"What is that?" Kai asked.

"It's Japanese, maneki-neko, a beckoning cat. They're used by merchants and restaurant owners to bring luck and money and beckon the passerby to come inside," he explained.

Given the influx of immigrants to the islands it was not a surprise to find a maneki-neko on the island, but Tex certainly would never have thought to find one here.

"The skull warns us to keep away while the cat beckons us to come closer. There's a mixed message for you," he said drily.

"I do not like this," Kai said. "What does it mean?"

The skull represented death. However, it might have a meaning beyond the standard "keep out" message those things were often meant to convey. It could be a symbol of the goblet itself, thus an indication that they were in the right place.

The cat's meaning was perfectly clear, though. He put his satchel down on the ground.

"It means that it's time to go on in," Tex said, bending to relieve himself of his boots.

"I do not know what might be in that pond," Kai said, alarm clear in his voice.

"Isn't that part of the fun?" Tex looked more closely at the cat. "I think he's pointing."

"Pointing at a couple of fools. Time to give up."

"Never," Tex hissed. He had come too far to give up now. He turned and dropped into the pond, plunging beneath the waters. The temperature was colder than he had anticipated. That was likely owing to the fact that the pond was somewhat screened from the tropical sun by the dense coconut grove.

The water stung his eyes when he opened them. It was too dark to really make anything out. He moved his hands against the packed earth that was keeping the water in the pond prisoner, searching for something that seemed out of place. His hands brushed against tree roots and coconut husks. All to be expected.

Then his hand brushed against something rough with ridges and rounded edges. He seized hold of it and tried to lift it free. Whatever it was proved too heavy and he finally had to go up for air.

"Help me, there's something down here," he said.

A moment later Kai splashed into the water next to him. That was the thing with Hawaiians, they spent more time in the water than anyone else Tex had ever met. It was second nature to them.

This time Tex was able to brace his foot against a root protruding from the bank. Together they heaved and were able to bring the object to the surface of the water. Tex held it afloat while Kai scrambled out and together they got it onto solid ground.

It was a giant clam shell.

"What on earth was that doing in there?" Kai asked.

Tex got out of the water and squatted down beside it. "Someone put it there for safekeeping," he said as he examined it more carefully.

Kai just shook his head.

"When you build your hotel you should use clamshells as the sinks," Tex said.

Kai wrinkled up his nose. "I don't think that would be easy to do."

"Trust me; it would be worth it."

"Maybe someday you'll retire and buy a hotel. Then you can do with it what you like."

Tex reached into his bag and took out his trowel. He found a spot where he could insert it in between the two halves of the shell. He applied pressure downward and the top of the shell began to move. He was able to grab hold of it and open it the rest of the way.

Inside there was a faded piece of kapa cloth wrapped around something. Tex picked it up and slowly unwrapped the object inside. When at last the cloth fell away he was holding a small, rough hewn cup with hideous, distorted faces carved all the way around it.

Tex touched it and felt a shiver dart up his spine. He had a sudden sick feeling deep inside that he struggled to ignore. It was just the legends about the cup that were working on his imagination, conjuring up horrific thoughts and feelings. It had no basis in fact.

"This is what it's all about," he muttered and began to wrap it back up. It was then that he noticed a smaller piece of cloth. He set everything down on his satchel and then unwrapped the smaller bit of cloth.

Inside it was a small gem, shaped like a teardrop. It was dark hued, almost black but with a kind of purple glow to it. He reached out his hand to touch it. Where he expected it to be cool to the touch it was instead warm. Tex had never seen anything like it.

Something about it tugged at him, as though he were trying to remember a long forgotten dream. Slowly things became clearer and he realized that the gem looked like something he might have heard about once in a lecture. He stared at it for another moment, transfixed. It couldn't possibly be what he thought it was.

"What is that?" Kai asked.

"Something that shouldn't exist," Tex muttered. He quickly wrapped it back up and shoved it in his pocket. "What's important, though, is that we got what we came for."

He stood and picked up both the sacred cup and the satchel. "It's time to go home."

He put the cup in its cloth wrapping into the satchel, eager to not have to touch it anymore. His mind, though, was on the gem in his pocket. It had been in one of Dr. Reid's classes that he'd heard a legend about teardrop shaped gems such as that one. Dr. Reid was a bit of a riddle himself. The man always lectured his classes about not jumping to conclusions and about taking myths and legends with a large grain of salt. Yet, despite his many rants against what he called para-archaeology, he knew everything there was to know about mythology. Tex had long suspected that Dr. Reid was actually more believer than skeptic. Whatever his beliefs, it was well-known that his knowledge of antiquity was beyond compare. If you were chasing down legends like the cup or the teardrop gems, he was the guy you'd want to talk to.

"You never know what you're going to find until you find it," Tex muttered.

That had always been Dr. Reid's favorite saying. That theory had actually proven itself out in the field time and time again.

"You seem troubled. Are you not happy to have the object of your search in your hands?" Kai asked.

"I am," Tex said. Although truth be told he'd be much happier once the artifact was *out* of his hands. There was a deep level of satisfaction in the finding of such an object.

There was an infinitely deeper level of satisfaction in making it home alive and turning it into someone else's problem.

Fortunately this expedition already had a backer, someone who had shown more interest in acquiring the ceremonial cup than they had much of anything else in the past few years. That was Nathaniel, though. He always went in for the weird items. The creepier the better.

There was a sudden, loud banging sound and the earth shook violently beneath his feet throwing him onto the ground. He barely managed to twist his body in time so that he didn't land on top of the satchel and its prize. Next to him Kai hit the ground as well, his eyes wide in terror.

A coconut landed inches from Tex's head. He shielded the satchel with his body and then covered his head with his arms, knowing that if one of those coconuts hit him in the head it would almost certainly kill him.

"We have angered the gods. They are trying to kill us!" Kai shouted. "We must put the goblet back where you found it."

"This has nothing to do with gods or goblets. This is an earthquake! It will stop in a few sec-" Tex broke off, hissing in agony as a coconut smashed against his left arm. Pain seared through him and he knew the arm was broken.

The irony was it was the same arm that had been broken when he experienced his first earthquake as a very young child. He and his aunt had survived the 1906 quake in San Francisco although their house had partially collapsed and later been destroyed entirely by the fires that swept through the city.

Digging in the pile of debris several days later and feeling the wild joy of discovering a favorite toy thought lost forever had honestly been what started him on the path of archaeology. So, that earthquake was responsible for him being here during this earthquake. He just hoped the irony didn't kill him.

The earth stopped shaking at last and he got up slowly, fighting the urge to clutch his broken arm and instead using his good hand to pick up his satchel. That had been a close one.

He turned and looked at Kai who was still prostrate on the ground. "Are you okay?" he asked.

Kai looked up at him slowly, eyes full of fear. "No thanks to you. You must put the cup back, exactly where you found it."

"That's not going to happen," Tex said. "The two events have nothing in common. It's just unfortunate timing."

Kai stood slowly to his feet. Tex could see that the other man was shaking. It was probably his first earthquake, and while Tex didn't blame him for being frightened by it, he wouldn't suffer silly superstitions to get in his way.

"Come on. There's a plane bound for Oahu tonight and I intend to be on it."

"Not with the cup you won't be." Kai took a step forward menacingly.

"Come on, Kai. I like you. I'm going to stay at your hotel when you build it, remember?"

Kai lunged forward, trying to grab the satchel and Tex twisted out of the other man's reach. "Kai, be reasonable."

Kai pulled a hunting knife out of a sheath he wore on his belt.

"That is definitely not reasonable," Tex muttered as he went into a fighting stance. He'd only have one good chance to end this before one of them got killed.

He swung the satchel up underneath his left arm and hissed sharply as pain radiated out through the arm. It left his right hand free, though. Kai lunged forward and Tex was able to grab his wrist and twist it such that the other man dropped the knife.

Quick as a flash Tex snatched up the knife, flipped it over in his hand, and threw it so that the butt end hit Kai squarely in the head. The guide went down hard. Tex tarried a moment to make sure that he was still breathing, then he set out through the coconut grove.

It was five miles to the airport but with pain shooting up his arm at every step he took it might as well be a hundred miles. He stuck to the fields. It made the walking slower, more jarring to his arm, but he couldn't risk Kai or one of his friends finding him on the road. As it was he heard only three cars drive by him.

He reached what passed for an airport on the island at last. He could see the plane on the tarmac that would be carrying passengers to Honolulu. He carefully surveyed his surroundings, wary of any possible traps. He could see no one out of the ordinary, though.

He finally made a dash for the plane and was halfway up the stairs before pausing to look behind him. Fortunately no one seemed to be giving chase. He climbed the rest of the way inside and met the startled eyes of the stewardess.

"This flight is full," she said.

"I have a reservation. Ravencroft."

She checked her manifest. “Yes, Dr. Ravencroft. You’re the last to arrive. We were beginning to think we’d be taking off without you.”

“Trust me, I was worried about that, too,” he admitted.

He took his seat, stowing his satchel under the seat in front of him. He began to relax when the stewardess sealed up the door. Usually he took flights as a perfect opportunity to update his journal. With his arm the way it was, though, he was just hoping that he would pass out instead. Fortunately the flight wouldn’t be a long one and then he could see a Doctor on Oahu who could fix him up.

His journal was tucked safely away in his satchel along with his finds and there it would stay for a while. He’d have to record the day’s events in it soon. He made a habit of keeping notes on his adventures though no eyes but his ever read them. Good archaeologists took extensive notes at every dig site to do their best to record what they found so others might later study the information. He’d gotten into the habit of taking those detailed notes when training on his first dig site. His activities that were a little beyond the pale also came in for the same treatment though he wasn’t sure he was doing himself a service by recording some of his more questionable activities.

He sighed as he leaned his head back. Things had been going so well earlier. Why did they so often have to take a turn for the worse. It was a lovely island. Too bad he wouldn’t be staying at Kai’s hotel after all.

Chapter 2

Tex breathed a little easier as soon as the plane was in the air. Once they were in Honolulu he would go to the hospital and have his arm looked at. He could tell that it was broken. Hopefully he could get a cast and get on his way quickly so he could book passage on a ship heading to California. From California he'd head back east by train. All-in-all it would take him a couple of weeks to make it to Washington D.C. where he would be able to unburden himself of the ceremonial goblet in his satchel.

This was the part that he always hated. The thrill of the hunt, figuring out where something was and going off to find it always invigorated him. Someone had once told him he wasn't happy unless he was chasing something. Maybe that was true. He also enjoyed the moment of discovery, though, the successful end of the hunt. Then came the hard part, though. Once he had an item such as the goblet in his possession he felt the need to be even more cautious and paranoid than before he had it.

His greatest fear was losing the prize once he had it. Once when he was young and naive someone had stolen something from him, and he had vowed never to let it happen again. So now the watching and endless waiting set in as he became more and more anxious to deliver his find and get paid for it.

Private collectors would pay big money for antiquities from all over the globe, especially if a man was discreet and allowed them to take the credit for the discovery. However, Tex had always preferred to work with museums. He hadn't encountered a treasure yet that wasn't best shared with the world. Fortunately, he knew curators from half a dozen institutions that agreed with him and were willing to pay him for the things he found.

Probably his strongest relationship these days was with Nathaniel Grant who worked in acquisitions at the Smithsonian Institution. In fact, it was Nathaniel who had sent him after this particular piece which he had heard rumors of and was dying to add to the Smithsonian's collection.

It was the first time Nathaniel had ever asked him to find something specific. Hawaiian antiquities were outside of Tex's area of expertise, but he enjoyed a good challenge and doing this favor for Nathaniel could only strengthen their relationship. It also didn't hurt that the man was offering him quite a tidy sum to retrieve the goblet. Which didn't help his paranoia at the moment.

He kept glancing at the handful of other passengers, wondering what their stories were. It was a game he used to play as a child where he would try to figure out who people were, what they did for a living, and other details just by observing them. More than once as an adult his old childhood game had saved his life.

Fortunately, none of his fellow passengers on the flight seemed suspicious. He tried to force himself to relax, and he let his mind drift to the tear-shaped gem in his pocket. One of his professors at college, Dr. Reid, had been giving a lecture on the relationship between mythology and archaeology. Several of the other professors had been scandalized because Dr. Reid deigned to mention myths of the holy grail, a universal flood, and a lost continent with a straight face. Even Tex had thought the good doctor had gone a little overboard on that one. Dr. Reid was a legend in his field, though, and legends needed to be accorded some degree of respect whether you agreed with them or not.

Of course, it was impossible to overstate the influence Dr. Reid had had on him. When Tex had been one of his students he had plans to travel the world adventuring after graduation and never settle down in any one place. In the end he had followed the older man's example. Tex had become a college professor, teaching about history and antiquities. The schedule gave him time off to still go on archaeological digs and his own personal quests. The fact that universities practically begged for you to further your own education, write papers, and take sabbaticals made it difficult to argue with the advantages of working there. It also gave him access to some of the finest library collections in the world which made research so much easier. The steady pay didn't hurt either.

When he finally landed in Honolulu his arm was hurting badly enough that just moving in the slightest was enough to make him grit his teeth in anguish. Fortunately it wasn't far from the airport to the hospital. The admissions nurse took one look at his rapidly swelling arm and immediately got him into a room.

He was asked to take off his shirt which he carefully folded inside his satchel, careful to make sure the gem was safely tucked away.

About ten minutes later a young Hawaiian doctor came in. He extended his hand which Tex shook.

"I'm Dr. Robinson."

"Tex Ravencroft."

"Broke your arm?" the doctor asked.

"Yes."

The doctor picked up his injured arm and Tex winced. The man began examining it. "Tex is an unusual name," he said conversationally.

"It's a nickname," he answered, trying not to grunt in pain as the doctor felt the bones in his arm.

"Are you from Texas?"

"No."

"Did you go to school there?"

"No."

"Then how did you get the nickname?"

"I don't think it-"

The doctor pulled his arm straight and Tex gave a strangled yell.

"Okay, it seems like a clean break. We'll get you in a cast and on your way," Dr. Robinson said.

Tex stared at him. "You didn't care how I got my nickname."

"No, I just wanted to take your mind off what I was doing for a second," Dr. Robinson said with a flash of teeth. "So, how did you break your arm?"

"Falling coconut."

"For real?" the doctor asked with a squint.

"Yes."

"Were you trying to catch it or something?"

"No, I was busy covering my head."

"Lucky. Wouldn't want your head smashed like this."

"That was my thought process."

A couple hours later Tex made it back to the hotel room he had been staying in before his trip to Kauai. Normally he tried to record his activities in his journal at the end of each day, but it was going to have to wait. He barely managed to sit down on the bed before the pain and exhaustion overtook him and he passed out.

He woke suddenly several hours later. He stayed absolutely still as he tried to figure out what had woken him. The pain in his arm was sharp, but he'd slept with worse. No, something had disturbed him. Maybe it was something he'd heard? He strained his ears, listening for anything. There was nothing. He took a slow, deep breath trying to calm himself.

That was when it hit him. He could smell mint very strongly in his room. There had been no such scent earlier.

Slowly he opened his eyes the slightest bit, straining to see if he could make out anything. The room was dark but to his right he could vaguely see the silhouette of a man. He caught a flash of movement and he rolled out of the way just as a knife came down and slashed the mattress where he had been.

Tex fell off the bed, trying not to land on his injured arm. His gun and knife were both in his satchel which was on the table by the window. He scrambled across the floor as behind him he heard a man curse in a language he was unfamiliar with.

He had just reached the table when he felt a sharp stinging in his right temple. Just in front of him the assailant's knife lodged into the wall. As blood began to roll down his cheek Tex managed to grab the satchel and yank out the gun. He turned and fired two shots. The first one missed, but the second struck flesh.

There was a flash of movement and then the door to his room was flung wide and a tall man ran into the hall. Tex pulled himself to his feet and ran after him, but by the time he got to the door the man had vanished. Up and down the hall other doors were opening and people were sticking their heads out. He hid his gun behind his back and eased back into his room.

He flicked on the light switch. It was time to get out of here. In five minutes he could be packed and ready. He could do it in one if he decided to leave behind his clothes and toiletries. There was a reason he never gave his real name when he checked into a hotel. Unpleasantness always seemed to happen.

He walked toward the table and stopped. There, on the bed near the spot where it had been slashed, was a small card about the size of a calling card. It wasn't his, so his attacker must have dropped it.

Cautiously he picked it up and turned it over. On the back of the card secured by a clear covering was a yellow flower. He didn't know right off what it was or what the significance of it could be. There were no other markings of any sort on the card, but he could detect a faint whiff of mint.

He put the card in his satchel along with the goblet. He turned and went to the closet to grab his suitcase and less than five minutes later he was poking his head out into the hall. A hotel employee was at the far end talking with some people in one of the rooms. There was no way of leaving out his door without being seen.

He was three stories up. Behind him was a sliding glass door that led onto a small balcony. On another day he might have opted to go over and climb down, jumping from balcony to balcony. With his arm in the cast there was no way he could pull that off.

So, he'd have to bluff his way out.

He walked out of his room with his bags, slamming the door behind him. At the far end of the hallway the hotel employee, who looked like he was probably the manager, jumped. Other guests who were lurking in their doorways did as well. "I thought this was a respectable establishment!" Tex raved, putting as much fear and anger into his voice as he could.

"I'm checking out right now before whoever that was starts shooting again. Who's with me?"

A couple of people started nodding their heads. The manager hurried his way. "I assure you, this is a respectable hotel. We've never had anything like this happen before," the man said, his voice distressed.

"How can it be respectable when your guests are woken in the middle of the night by gunshots?" Tex demanded.

"Who was it?" a woman across the hall piped up.

"Are the police on their way?" another man questioned.

The manager raised his hands. "Everyone, I can assure you that we are doing what we can to get to the bottom of this and ensure the safety of our guests."

Now other guests were crowding into the hall, forming a circle around the manager. Some were demanding answers, others refunds. The poor man would have his hands full for a while.

Tex took the opportunity to head straight for the stairwell. Down in the lobby there were a few frightened guests milling around. Police entered just as he got there. Tex turned and made his way to the back of the hotel where there was a service entrance he had scouted when he first arrived.

Two minutes later he was on the streets which were almost entirely deserted. A couple of drunken sailors waved to him, and a bum threw an empty bottle his way when he accidentally woke the man up.

As he walked he kept an eye out for his unseen attacker. Had the man known who he was or had he just been a random victim? He was inclined to believe the former. People usually didn't sneak into hotel rooms in the middle of the night to knife a stranger with no reason. Maybe Kai had sent one of his cousin's after Tex.

One thing was for sure. He'd worn out his welcome, and it was time for him to leave while he still could.

Chapter 3

On his journey back home no one else tried to kill Tex which he was grateful for, but he spent the time consumed with worry about the things he had in his possession and questions regarding two of them. He still puzzled over the tear-shaped gem, but his paranoia about having something lost or stolen was great enough that he left it secure inside his satchel.

On the other hand, the card with the yellow flower on it that his would-be assassin had left in his room he pulled out frequently to study. He still hadn't been able to detect anything about it, but it bothered him. Leaving some sort of calling card seemed more like something a Jack the Ripper type killer would do. Still, he couldn't shake the belief that the man had targeted him deliberately either for who he was or for what he had. The questions had nearly driven him mad by the time he returned home.

He made it to his small house near The George Washington University in the evening. It was too late to call on Nathaniel or Dr. Reid so he had to hold on to the goblet and his questions for another night.

After showering and settling in he took the satchel to his study. There he carefully unwrapped the gem for the first time since he'd left Hawaii. He set it carefully on his desk and retrieved a magnifying glass to observe it more closely. The blackish-purple gem was about the size of a fingernail.

Even using the magnifying glass he couldn't detect anything new about it.

Finally he reached out and touched it to turn it over. It was still warm to the touch just like when he'd found it. He kept it between his fingers for a moment, studying the edges. Again he saw nothing, but he did become aware that the gem seemed to be getting warmer.

He turned it over and set it down. He let his fingers linger on it for a moment more, fascinated by the apparent growing warmth from it. He realized he had to be imagining it. There was no way the heat from his body should be causing it to warm that quickly.

Then suddenly the gem seemed to shimmer for a moment and fire red hues appeared in its depths. He removed his fingers so he could see the whole of it and in almost an instant the color had faded back to its original blackish-purple.

He studied it closely with the magnifying glass, tilting his head first one way and then another. Perhaps it was similar to an opal and the fire appeared best at certain angles. Try as he did, though, he couldn't find a way to look at it that showed even a hint of the red hue.

Frustrated he picked it up, planning to turn it over again. The gem began to heat up and he hesitated. He held it, letting it rest in the palm of his hand and he watched through the magnifying glass. Several seconds later it seemed to come back to life again, red spreading throughout the gem. It started to glow brighter and brighter and he realized that the brighter it glowed the hotter it got. At last he couldn't stand it any longer and had to drop it back on his desk. The red immediately began to fade. On the palm of his hand where it had been resting there was a small, tear-shaped burn mark now visible.

How was any of this possible?

He had a feeling he knew what Dr. Reid was going to say, but Tex was hoping there was a logical answer to the mystery. He carefully wrapped the gem back up and tucked it into his satchel.

The next afternoon it was with considerable relief that Tex sat down across from Nathaniel Grant in the latter's office inside the Castle, the Smithsonian Institution's administrative offices. He'd arrived in the morning, but had been told that Nathaniel had just returned from vacation and was in meetings all morning. He had opted to wait, not wanting to travel more than necessary until he had gotten rid of the goblet. At last he was called into Nathaniel's office.

Nathaniel was one of the men tasked with making acquisitions on behalf of the museum. He was a tall, slender man with red hair and intense brown eyes that often unnerved lesser men. Fortunately, Tex had known Nathaniel long enough and been subjected to that stare often enough that it didn't bother him.

"So, what do you have for me?" Nathaniel asked without preamble.

"Good to see you, too," Tex said.

Nathaniel leaned back in his chair and sighed. "Sorry, it's been one of those weeks. You know how it is."

"And since when was vacation so rough?"

He grimaced. "It was more of a working vacation. I know you know how those go."

Tex nodded stiffly and refused to glance at the cast on his left arm which had been itching him like crazy for the last few days.

"Glad to see that you seem to be in one piece, well, mostly," Nathaniel said with his customary dry wit.

"As long as I brought you something back from my trip, I'm guessing you could care less what condition I'm in," Tex said.

"I would say that was more than a tad unfair. You know I'm always concerned about your safety."

Tex reached into his satchel on the floor, pulled out the kapa cloth wrapped goblet, and set it on Nathaniel's desk.

The curator's eyes grew wide as he stared at it for a moment without moving. "Is it?" he asked at last.

"See for yourself."

Slowly Nathaniel stretched out his hands toward it as though hesitant to touch it. Given his obvious excitement Tex found his actions strange and he sat up slightly, watching the other man more closely. What was it about this cup that had gotten under Nathaniel's skin?

With his fingertips a mere inch from it, Nathaniel pulled back suddenly.

Tex raised an eyebrow. "You want me to do the honors?"

"No, no. I just don't want to damage it," Nathaniel said, reaching into his desk. He pulled out a pair of gloves and slipped them on. Finished, he reached out and took hold of the cup. He unfolded the fabric, exposing the goblet, but Tex was quick to note that Nathaniel kept the cloth between it and his gloved hand.

"You don't believe all those crazy stories, do you?" he asked. It would explain the man's hesitation to touch it directly.

Tex had to admit that after touching it the first time, he'd avoided it since. He didn't care to have a repeat of the sensations he had experienced, even if he didn't believe the cup held supernatural power. It had still been used in human sacrifices, and that was disturbing enough to not want to be too close to it.

"One man's crazy story is another man's truth," Nathaniel mused. "Who are we to say what is and what isn't?"

"That what you're going to print on the display plaque?"

"Pardon?"

"I assume you wanted the cup for an exhibit."

"Oh...yes, a very special exhibit," Nathaniel said.

He was lying, Tex felt it in his bones. But it made no sense. Why else would Nathaniel have wanted to pay him for securing the cup? If it had been somebody else Tex might have suspected that he had wanted it to sell on the black market where an artifact like the cup could fetch a pretty penny. Nathaniel had made his feelings on the secret buying and selling of antiquities well-known in the past, though. So, it couldn't be that unless something had happened to change his mind.

They say every man has a price. Maybe someone had found Nathaniel's. When such a thin line separated archaeology and grave robbing it wasn't surprising that many ended up on the other side at some point or another. He himself had straddled that line on a couple of occasions.

"As long as you're not planning on using it in any blood rituals, cannibalism, that sort of thing," Tex said wryly.

"What would make you think that?" Nathaniel said, clearly not getting the joke.

"You know the ancient Greeks thought people with red hair turned into vampires after they died."

"Very funny," Nathaniel said.

"The last time I was over here I spent some time walking around and looking at the exhibits in the museum. Found a lot of...shall we say...discrepancies?"

Nathaniel just waved his hand dismissively. "Truth varies from different people's perspectives."

"Yes, but facts are facts and the museum has gotten a few of them wrong."

"Did you find anything else with it?" Nathaniel asked suddenly.

"No, should I have?" Tex asked. He could not be made to give up the existence of the teardrop shaped gem until he knew more about it.

"No," Nathaniel said, eyes still fixed on the cup. At last he wrapped it back up and placed it on a shelf behind him. He took off the gloves and returned them to their drawer from which he also produced an envelope that he put down on the desk between them.

"You'll find the rest of your payment in there," he said.

Tex took the envelope and put it in his interior coat pocket.

"So, what's next for you? Are you off on another quest or heading back to the classroom?"

"I'm not sure," Tex admitted. In truth a lot would depend on what he learned when he met with Dr. Reid.

“If you’re in need of work, I’m sure I could throw a few more projects your way.”

“I might take you up on that. Once I get the cast off, of course.”

“Of course. Best to heal up before tackling anything new.”

“Truer words were never spoken,” Tex said, standing up and offering his hand.

Nathaniel stood as well and shook. “Always a pleasure.”

Tex left the building still thinking about the meeting with Nathaniel and what the other man planned to do with the cup. Ultimately it wasn’t his concern, but the whole meeting had seemed slightly off to him, particularly the part where Nathaniel wondered if he had found anything else with the cup.

Tex was eager to speak with Dr. Reid. He headed for the university where Dr. Reid also taught, hoping to catch the man in his office. When he got there he was disappointed to learn that Dr. Reid wasn’t there. He debated for a moment what to do next. A sudden thought occurred to him and he headed for a different building.

Fortunately Dr. Calhoun was in. He looked up from his cluttered desk and waved enthusiastically to Tex. “Come in!”

Tex entered and sat down across from him. Dr. Calhoun was a renowned botanist and he might just be able to answer some of Tex’s other questions.

“What happened to your arm?” he asked.

“Hit by a falling coconut,” Tex said, knowing it would amuse the other man.

"Those things can be dangerous," Dr. Calhoun said, eyes lighting up. "That's why I put coconut palms on my list of killer vegetation for the lecture I give to first year students."

"Well, now you can tell them that you actually know someone who was injured by one. It nearly killed me. Would have if my arm hadn't been covering my head."

"Really?" Dr. Calhoun asked, sounding much too excited about that prospect. The man needed to get out more.

"Yes. Dr. Calhoun, I was wondering if you could help me identify a particular flower?"

"I shall do my best," he said.

Tex pulled the card with the flower out of his satchel and handed it over.

Dr. Calhoun took it and studied it eagerly for a few moments before handing it back to Tex.

"Do you know what it is?" Tex asked as he put the card back in his satchel.

"Oh yes, it's Helenium autumnale."

Tex sighed. "What's it's common name?"

"Most call it sneezeweed."

"Sneezeweed?"

"Yes. Also Helen's flower and dogtooth daisy."

"Colorful names," Tex noted.

"They are, aren't they?"

"What else can you tell me about them?"

"Native to North America. The Iroquois used to make a sort of snuff out of them to relieve headaches by forcing sneezing."

"Hence the name sneezeweed."

"Precisely. It's also named Helen's flower after Helen of Troy. It was said that these were the flowers that were formed from her tears when she wept when kidnapped."

"I thought she went with Paris willingly?"

"Depending on who you listen to. Either way she was kidnapped by someone else as a child. Of course, that's nonsense about the flowers being formed from her tears."

"Because the supernatural doesn't exist," Tex said.

Dr. Calhoun blinked at him. "No, because these flowers weren't in ancient Greece."

"Right, of course," Tex said struggling to keep the sarcasm from his voice. "Do you know of any groups who might use this flower as a symbol?" he asked.

It was a stab in the dark, but he had nothing to lose.

Dr. Calhoun blinked for a moment as though thinking rapidly. "I'm sorry, I can't think of ever hearing about anyone using this flower for a group symbol."

"That's okay, it was a longshot," Tex said. The truth was the card was likely just the calling card for that one men or for a very small, criminal group. He'd be shocked if Dr. Calhoun would know anything about that kind of organization.

"Is there anything more?" Dr. Calhoun asked.

"No, thank you for your time. I really appreciate it."

"Always happy to do a colleague a favor."

"If there's anything else you can think of that's significant about this flower, I'd appreciate you letting me know," Tex said.

Dr. Calhoun nodded solemnly.

"Do you know where I might find Dr. Reid?" he asked.

"He's almost always at the library, I believe. I haven't seen him around in several days. Or maybe it's been weeks."

"Thanks."

At least now he knew where to find Dr. Reid. Given how late it was, though, he would probably have to meet him the next day. Usually downtime was a welcome relief, but in this case curiosity was eating him alive. It was more than that, though, he kept having this feeling deep inside like there was an invisible clock ticking away, counting down to...something.

Regardless, his was a waiting game at the moment. That didn't mean, though, that it wasn't a good time to brush up on his Plato.

Tex made it to the door and was about to leave when the other man called after him.

"There is one other thing."

"What?" Tex asked, turning.

"It's nothing much, and fairly obvious once you understand the different names of the flower, but in the language of flowers which has been used at different points in history as a sort of secondary form of communication it has a specific meaning."

"And what's that?"

"Because of the myth about Helen, the flower represents a tear."

Chapter 4

As Tex left the university and headed home his mind was racing. It had to be a coincidence that the flower left by the man who had attacked him meant tear and that the gem he had recovered was shaped like a teardrop. His mind was leaping to preposterous conclusions. It didn't help, though, that he believed that the tear was connected to a Greek myth.

Later that evening at home, after thumbing through the pertinent parts of the Timaeus and Critias, he again pulled out the stone to look at it. He spent half the evening running mini experiments on it. Although it heated quickly when in contact with flesh and cooled when isolated, it didn't seem to respond to anything else. He tried placing it against wood, various types of metals, glass, and plastic. There was no response. After thinking about it for a while he tried placing it against leather to see if the skin of an animal had any affect.

Nothing. It remained its same dark hue. In frustration he sat back, trying to figure out why it only responded to his touch. At last he finally gave up and went to bed, hoping that Dr. Reid would have some answers.

The next morning he headed over to the library. The library, which was on the university grounds, was world-renowned for its collection of ancient manuscripts. Everyone knew it was one of Dr. Reid's favorite places to be, surrounded by the intrigue and mystery of thousands of years of human history.

Tex walked through the library, heading for a table in the back, far corner where only those wishing to be undisturbed went. There, sitting at a table at the far back, was Dr. Reid. From the looks of the stacks of books piled on the table and around it he had already been there for some time. The man had dark hair and blue eyes that were a lighter shade than Tex's. He was wearing a tweed jacket over his shirt and he could not have looked any more like a professor than he did. Next to him, propped against the table, was a mahogany walking stick. The professor walked with a distinct limp that Tex had heard was the result of a rafting accident years before.

In Dr. Reid's lap, purring and staring up at Tex, was the black cat that went everywhere with the man. Back at school the joke had been that the cat was Dr. Reid's familiar. The animal squinted its yellow eyes as though sizing Tex up. Then he made a little chirping sort of noise which got the attention of his master.

Dr. Reid looked up and then smiled. "Charles, good to see you."

Tex winced. The professor was the only one who called him that. No one else dared.

"You're looking well, Professor."

"Can't complain. You look a bit worse for wear, though."

Tex grimaced at his cast. "Arm will be good as new in a couple more weeks. What are you researching?"

"Anything and everything."

"I believe that there is more knowledge crammed into your head than a library twice this size could hold."

Dr. Reid chuckled. "You flatter me, but tell me why you're here. Surely it's not to find out what my current reading interests are?"

Tex sat down on the opposite side of the table and leaned forward. "Actually, I'm here because of something I found a few weeks ago. I wanted your opinion on it."

"That does sound intriguing. Shall we have a look at it then?" he asked, a grin on his face.

Tex pulled the piece of cloth out of his satchel. He set it on the table and unwrapped it until the gem was exposed.

Almost instantly the grin disappeared from Dr. Reid's face. His pupils actually seemed to dilate as he leaned forward and stared intently at the gem. He reached forward, but didn't touch the gem. Instead he tugged the piece of cloth it was sitting on closer to him. Even his cat was busy trying to get a better look.

"Where did you find this?" he asked, his voice strained.

"On Kauai. It was hidden with a ceremonial goblet that was used in human sacrifice rituals." He left off the supposed supernatural aspects of the cup. He didn't believe in them and odds were good the professor would already know of them anyway.

"What happens when you touch it?"

"It heats up fast, and becomes too hot to hold while also starting to turn a red color."

He nodded like he wasn't surprised by the answer. He reached out finally and put a finger on the gem. Moments later he removed it. "You're right, of course," he said softly.

"It only seems to respond to human touch," Tex said.

"Hmmm, we'll see about that," Dr. Reid mused.

A moment later, as though understanding the entire conversation, the cat reached out its paw and touched the gem. When it started to turn red the cat pulled his paw back.

"So, it responds to living creatures," Dr. Reid noted. "It's possible it's making some sort of connection with the electrical systems in the human body."

It sounded insane, but it was a better theory than any Tex had been able to come up with.

"Before we send it off to Edison for study, do you have any idea what it is?"

"I have one theory, but you're not going to like it."

"I already guessed that."

"Of course you did. Why else would you bring it to me? I don't believe this is a gemstone. I believe this is orichalcum," Dr. Reid said.

"As in the mythical metal used in Atlantis?"

"The very one."

"I was afraid you were going to say that," Tex admitted.

"So you already suspected the truth?"

"It has pretty unique properties."

"Yes, one theory has it that the metal could be used to generate more energy output than input."

"That's impossible. Doesn't that break some laws of physics?"

"No, but it certainly breaks some theories we currently hold about physics. We as a species are arrogant if we think we've solved all the mysteries of how the universe works."

Tex took a deep breath. "Okay, putting aside that discussion for the time being, let's say this is a piece of actual orichalcum from a real-life Atlantis. What on earth was a piece of it doing hidden on Kauai?" Tex asked.

"Perhaps the more interesting question is, why is this the first piece that has turned up?"

Tex rubbed his forehead. He could feel one of Dr. Reid's mind-bending, deeply questioning, truth challenging discussions coming. Those usually gave him a headache.

"Okay, why is it the first piece?"

Dr. Reid raised an eyebrow. "Maybe it is, and maybe it isn't. I believe the metal was fairly rare and highly prized. I wouldn't be surprised to find what few remnants might exist hiding out in private collections around the world, their owners likely unaware of exactly what marvels they hold. Still, the vast majority of orichalcum would have sank, along with Atlantis. A tragedy for sure. A metal with these properties must have a great many applications.

"Yes, but this is small and so distinctly shaped. What could someone have actually used it for?"

Dr. Reid hesitated for a moment as he seemed to be studying it. Finally, without lifting his eyes he said, "I believe that this is one of three Tears of Man."

"I've never heard of that."

"Very few have," Dr. Reid said. "There is a very old legend that there are three teardrop shaped bits of orichalcum that together help reveal the location of the sunken city of Atlantis."

"You're joking, right?"

"No."

"How exactly would the three Tears together do that?"

Dr. Reid just shook his head.

"Well, there definitely is something...different...about this, whatever it's made of," Tex said, touching the Tear briefly. "What can you tell me about Atlantis?"

"Not much more than what I assume you've already read for yourself in Plato's works."

Tex shook his head. "The blackish-purple color isn't from Plato's works. If I was going solely on his description I never would have recognized it. No, I remember you describing the color in a lecture you gave once on mythology."

"Good memory," he said with a smile. "However, Plato does say that the third outer wall of the citadel 'flashed with the red light of orichalcum'. You have certainly seen the red light from this stone."

"Yes, but even the name, orichalcum, derives from the Greek oreikhalkos which translates as mountain copper."

"Ah, but you are assuming, my dear Charles, that Greek was being spoken when the metal was given its name. Given the dates put forth for Atlantis it would be the metal orichalcum that came before the Greek language. Atlantis fell around 9,500 B.C. and the Greek language didn't come into existence for another 6,500 years after that. Therefore, it is much more probable that the Greek word oreikhalkos is derived from the name of the metal. And not the other way around. At any rate, Plato's tales are not the only place in antiquity where orichalcum is mentioned."

"None of that explains how you knew what color it was when at rest."

"A fragment of an ancient manuscript, tragically now lost, is what I was relying on in that lecture."

"Okay, say orichalcum exists, and even, that this is it," Tex said, indicating the Tear. "Do we actually believe that Atlantis existed?" Tex asked.

Dr. Reid just stared at him evenly. "What does this teardrop tell you? What have all your years in the field taught you?"

"That the world is a far more complicated place than we know."

"Exactly. From all over the world we find myths of lost continents or other civilizations."

"Proving that those kind of stories have a universal appeal to humans," Tex said.

"You sound like a textbook, and not a very imaginative one at that," Dr. Reid said with a sigh. "Is it not also possible that all these myths point to one great, cataclysmic event that reshaped the face of the ancient world and whose stories became zeitgeist?"

"You're talking now about the fall of Atlantis impacting the entire world."

"And why not? If they were an advanced culture. If they found a way to take this type of material and harness its power, then surely their influence could have been felt worldwide. Then, when Atlantis was destroyed, survivors could have been scattered throughout the world, taking some of the concepts and technology and designs with them, perpetuating the myths and helping to create some of the astonishing similarities we see between cultures which should have had no contact with one another."

Tex wasn't sure he was ready to jump on the Atlantis bandwagon, but he couldn't deny that the teardrop stone or metal or whatever it was didn't behave like anything he'd ever seen before. He also had never been able to turn his back on a good mystery.

"You asked where I found it. Why?"

Dr. Reid cleared his throat before continuing. "It has long been speculated that some survivors of Atlantis may have settled on various islands of Polynesia."

"Okay, would the other two Tears be located somewhere in Polynesia as well?" he asked.

"No, I do not believe so. Remember this culture was flung far and wide. I believe the other two Tears would have been separated from the first, for the protection of all."

Tex didn't even bother to ask the professor why he was drawing that particular conclusion. "Is there any indication where the other two might be located?" Tex asked.

"There are clues, but they are very vague. I have a few theories, though. If I'm right, they will not be as easy to obtain as this one was."

"You've been thinking about this for a long time," Tex noted.

The cat jumped onto the table and made his way over to a water glass and began to drink. Dr. Reid glanced around and then scooted his chair even closer to the table before leaning forward and lowering his voice.

"Are you familiar with the controversy revolving around the Grand Canyon and the Smithsonian Institution in 1909?"

"I can't say that I am."

"On April 5th of that year the Arizona Gazette ran a several page article about the ongoing exploration of an extensive cave system with Egyptian artifacts that was being conducted by the Smithsonian. The cave system had been discovered months before by an explorer."

"April 5th? That would be a bit late for an April Fool's joke."

"Indeed, though some have tried to claim it was just that. To this day the Smithsonian denies any involvement with the Grand Canyon and cave explorations."

Tex wondered what Nathaniel would have to say on the subject. It was before his time at the Smithsonian, but he might have heard something. He wasn't ready to bring Nathaniel into any of this, though. At least, not yet. Maybe later if the need arose. The man did have impressive resources at his disposal.

"So, what makes you think that this place exists and that if it does one of the other Tears might be there?"

"I saw a piece of a tablet once and the rough translation of it seemed to indicate that there was a group that left Egypt for a new land across the ocean and that their leader had taken the Tear with him."

"Where is this tablet?" Tex asked with a frown.

Dr. Reid sighed. "Alas, not in my possession. I can get my hands on it, but it will take some time and more than a little persuasion on my part to convince its keeper to share it."

"I have to say it feels like the whole thing is a legend, a ghost story, and you know I don't believe in ghosts."

"And what do you call this?" Dr. Reid asked, gesturing to the Tear on the table.

Tex reached out and touched it, feeling it begin to instantly heat up. "Proof of life after death," Tex admitted.

"I can get you a copy of the article in question. I can also give you some rough maps that I have acquired and made my own notes on. I have to warn you, though, the government owns that land and they don't let anyone near that location. You'd be trespassing."

"It wouldn't be the first time."

"And you'd risk getting shot."

"Wouldn't be the first time for that either."

Dr. Reid smiled. "I was hoping you'd see things that way."

The cat hissed and Dr. Reid quickly wrapped up the Tear and shoved it back at Tex.

"What is it?" Tex asked as he quickly stuffed it in his satchel.

"Someone's coming."

Chapter 5

Tex tensed every muscle in his body as he waited. He'd never seen Dr. Reid get that agitated about anything. Whoever was approaching couldn't be a friend. He heard a step, then another. He was halfway out of his chair, ready to attack if necessary.

A few seconds later a librarian appeared, spectacles on her nose and graying hair pulled into a tight bun. She grabbed a book from one of the shelves nearby and glared at the cat who glared back at her and hissed, showing its teeth. She disappeared, heading back toward the front of the library.

After a few moments the cat jumped back onto Dr. Reid's lap. It quickly began to purr.

"Some watchcat you have there," Tex said.

Dr. Reid smiled faintly as he stroked the feline's back. "Very much so. Now, where were we?"

"Arizona."

"Right. If you meet me back here tomorrow morning I can provide you with the papers that I mentioned."

"Then I'll plan to leave the day after tomorrow."

Dr. Reid nodded absently. "Just remember, be careful."

Tex grinned at him. "Where's the fun in that?"

Dr. Reid turned and pinned him with an intense stare that took Tex aback. Usually the professor enjoyed lighthearted banter. Something was different, though, because instead of smiling he leaned across the table.

"I'm telling you, be careful."

"I will," he said, his own smile rapidly fading.

He could feel a scratching at the back of his mind like some nagging thought that he knew was important but couldn't quite remember. Not good. That always meant he was walking into trouble.

He spent the rest of the day making arrangements for his travel out west. It was more than a little annoying that if he had only known when he was in Los Angeles what he knew now he might have saved himself a lot of time, travel, and expense. That was how it went, though.

After much debate he decided to take the train to Arizona and then, provided he found the second Tear, charter a plane back. He booked train passage for the following evening. It should give him plenty of time to collect the papers from Dr. Reid and pick up any last minute things he decided he needed. By the time he went to bed he was packed and ready to go.

The next morning he again found Dr. Reid in the library. This time his cat came over and rubbed his head on Tex's hand by way of greeting. Usually smiling, Dr. Reid was instead serious, his mannerisms quick and sharp. He handed Tex a thick envelope. "That's everything I can give you," he said.

"I appreciate it," Tex said as he took the envelope.

"I wish there was more I could do. I wish I could go with you."

"You've been a huge help already and you know I'm going to need your help again before this is all finished," Tex said with a cheery smile. "And you really don't want to go with me. Where I'm going wouldn't be safe for the cat."

Dr. Reid smiled faintly at that. He gestured to the cast Tex was still wearing. "What are you going to do about your arm?"

"I figure once I get to Arizona and get the lay of the land I'll get a sawbones there to cut me free."

"Is that wise?"

"No, but I'm sure it will be necessary," Tex said.

"You could delay your trip a week or two."

Tex quickly shook his head. "Now that I know what's out there I've got to go find it before someone else stumbles upon it."

"I doubt you have to worry too much about that."

"Ah, but you know me, professor, I do worry."

"As do I. More now than I used to."

Something occurred to Tex. Dr. Reid was practically a walking encyclopedia. He might know something about the Helenium flower. "Professor, have you heard about any group that uses the Helenium flower as its symbol or a sort of calling card?"

"The Helenium flower?" Dr. Reid asked, frowning slightly. "I'm not sure that I've heard of such a group. Why, did you encounter someone using that symbol?"

"Yes, and it just seemed odd. It was dropped by a man in Hawaii who tried to kill me."

Dr. Reid blanched. “Thank goodness he didn’t succeed.”

“I’m exceedingly grateful for that.”

“If I come across anything that might be helpful I’ll let you know.”

“I appreciate that, Professor.”

Take care of yourself, Charles.”

“I’ll see you in a couple of weeks,” Tex reassured him. He turned and walked away.

“Charles!”

He turned. Dr. Reid was looking at him. There was something he wanted to say, Tex could see that in his eyes and in the way he was holding himself. He stood up and came around the table, resting his hand lightly on its surface for support. “Make sure to take the first Tear with you. I would feel better knowing you were watching out for it. And, who knows, maybe you’ll need it for something.”

“I’m way ahead of you, professor,” Tex said. He patted his shirt pocket significantly.

Dr. Reid nodded. “Good luck to you,” he said, then bowed his head slightly.

“Thanks,” Tex said. Hopefully he wouldn’t need it.

As soon as he left the library he went back home. He quickly scanned through the documents in the envelope. It looked like he’d have plenty to read on the train during his three day trip. There was nothing left to do to get ready so he grabbed his bags and headed out for the train station.

Once there he sat, waiting for his train and trying not to stare suspiciously at anyone who wandered too close to him. He was hyper-aware of the Tear in his pocket and he started to think he would have been wiser to leave it with Dr. Reid. He smirked as he imagined it dangling on a collar around his cat's neck. It wouldn't stay there long, though, given the rate at which it heated up.

He kept telling himself to relax. There was no way anyone else could be on the trail of the Tears of Man. After all, no one but Dr. Reid knew he had discovered the first one. Anyone even remotely interested in the topic would have no reason to count it as anything other than myth at this point. That was how he wanted to keep it. He didn't need the competition. A lot of the amateurs who would be interested would just get in the way and inadvertently risk their lives and the safety of the artifacts he was going to be examining. The professionals who might want to jump into this fray were all too dangerous for him to want around and had a tendency not to want to share their findings. At least, not with the living.

He might be teaching future scientists who were interested in archaeology solely for academic purposes. Those who were currently in the field, though, knew full well that it was more about profit than anything else.

At last his train arrived and he hastily made his way to the sleeping compartment he had booked. He stowed his luggage and settled in. He had missed lunch and he was getting hungry. He knew he was being paranoid, but he didn't want to leave the papers that Dr. Reid had entrusted to him alone in the compartment. As soon as the train was moving he folded the envelope and secured it inside his jacket. After much debate he decided to wear his Colt M1911 in his shoulder holster underneath his tweed jacket, just in case. After he slipped his jacket back on, he headed to the dining car. Once there he sat down at an empty table and picked up his menu. He was only halfway through reading it when he heard a woman's voice above him.

"Is this seat taken?"

He looked up. A beautiful redhead was smiling down at him.

"No, it's not, would you care to join me," he said.

"Yes, thank you."

He rose and moved around the table to pull out the chair for her.

"Thank you, Mr. ..."

"Dr. Ravencroft."

"Dr. Ravencroft. It was very generous of you."

"Not at all, Mrs.-"

"Miss," she said with a coy smile. "Jenkins."

"Miss Jenkins, it's a pleasure to have your company this evening."

"Thank you."

She was quite attractive. She had large, green eyes a man could lose himself in, full, pouty lips, and her black dress accentuated her curves in all the right ways. He glanced around, noting that the other tables were filling up. Nowhere in the dining car was there a woman even half as attractive as she was. Apparently he had gotten lucky when it came to a dining companion.

"So, you are traveling alone as I am?" she asked.

"Yes. All the way to Los Angeles," he said, out of habit not telling her his actual destination.

"Then we shall enjoy several meals together. I am traveling to Phoenix," she offered.

"I am indeed the fortunate one at this table," he said with a smile.

Their waiter came over and they gave their food order. Once he had left she turned back to Tex with a dazzling smile. "So what do you do Dr. Ravencroft?"

"Please, call me Tex," he said. "Since we're going to be seeing so much of each other."

"Then you must call me Lena," she said.

"Alright, Lena. I teach history and archaeology."

Her large eyes widened even more. "Oh, that is fascinating. What a wonderful area of study."

"It has its rewards," he said, picking up his water glass and taking a sip.

"The past it's all so romantic to me."

"It can be easy to get caught up in its allure and mystery. There's so much we don't know. Our ancestors customs often seem strange to us and yet they were people just like we are with the same basic human needs and desires."

"And what do you see as the basic human needs and...desires?" she asked, her voice going a little breathy.

"Food, warmth, shelter, and someone to share them with."

She smiled, flashing perfect teeth. He had met women like her before. Beautiful, often rich, and willing to break the rules in pursuit of their hearts' desires, whatever those happened to be at the moment. He knew better than to fall into that trap. Besides, there was only one woman he wanted to share those things with.

And she had betrayed him and left him for dead.

He tried to shut out the memories that were starting to edge into his mind. He didn't need to think about that or *her* right now. Especially not when there was a young woman so eager to take his mind off everything.

"So, what's in Phoenix?" he asked as he put his glass down.

"My cousin. I'm going to stay with her for a couple of months."

"Well, I'm sure when you leave you'll be breaking a thousand hearts."

"I'd be happy to just once lose my heart to the right man."

She was flirting awfully hard. While it was not uncommon for women to flirt with him she was really working overtime. It made him suspicious that this was no casual attraction but that she wanted something from him.

"Tell me more about your work," she said.

"I do a lot of research, publish a paper or two a year, and teach classes. There's not much more to tell."

At least, not much more that he planned to tell her.

"Oh, come on, I'm sure it's all more complicated than that. Have you discovered anything exciting?"

She was definitely fishing. The question was, for what? In theory no one besides Dr. Reid knew that he had the Tear. The goblet had been handed off to Nathaniel. It was possible there was something else she wanted, something he'd had in the past or something she was hoping he'd help her get her hands on.

He narrowed his eyes. That had to be it. She was either a collector or, more likely, a go between for one. He was occasionally approached by private collectors who were wanting some relic or other and thought he was the man to get it for them.

"I'm afraid I'm just a boring old academic," he said.

She put a hand on top of his where it rested on the table. "Oh, I don't think there's anything boring or old about you," she purred.

He decided to stop beating around the bush and go with the direct approach. Maybe it would help him figure out exactly what, and who, he was dealing with.

"What is it you're wanting me to find for you?" he asked.

"Excuse me?" she asked, feigning naïveté.

"You heard archaeologist and you think there's something I can get you. One of Helen of Troy's jewels or perhaps something connected to Cleopatra."

"Both great beauties. Are you comparing me to them?" she asked, fluttering her eyelashes. "I'm sure I wouldn't mind."

But he would. He'd known only one woman who was worth going to war over. He picked up his water glass again, growing angry with himself for allowing the errant thoughts to blindside him like that.

"As a matter of fact, I do know someone who has a strong interest in the...rare and unusual," she said.

As he had expected.

"I don't steal for people."

"Oh, this wouldn't require stealing," she said, bothering to look hurt that he would make such a suggestion. "I mean, I would never be involved in-"

"What is it that he wants?" Tex said, no longer in the mood to play her games.

Before she could answer the waiter brought their food.

"Oh my, this all looks delicious," she said. "It's a shame to waste such a lovely dinner on boring business talk. Don't you think?"

He forced himself to smile. "Then perhaps we should focus on pleasure before business."

"I'll drink to that," she said, raising her glass.

He had a feeling she would.

The food turned out to be quite good, better than what he'd had on the eastbound train a few days before. Lena savored every bite as though it were her last. Most men would have found it stimulating. He just found it to be overly contrived. Still, he forced himself to make polite conversation.

It was swiftly evident that there really was no cousin in Phoenix that she was going to see. And whoever the collector she would ultimately be bargaining on behalf of, she had done it before. Given her confidence he was sure that she was used to getting what she wanted regardless of what it was or who it hurt. All the more reason to be wary of her.

When they had finally finished eating he excused himself and headed back to his compartment. He was tired, but he was determined to at least start going through the packet that Dr. Reid had given him before calling it a night. Of course, given how out of it he was feeling it would probably just be wasted effort because he'd have to reread everything in the morning anyway.

That was okay. He'd get through what he could of it before turning in and then it could simmer overnight in his subconscious. He did some of his best work that way and often awoke with fresh insights he would never have reached any other way.

He finally reached his compartment. He opened the door, started to take a step inside, and then froze. Clothes were strewn all over and the bed had been torn apart.

His compartment had been ransacked.

Chapter 6

Tex got off at the next stop for just a minute to use the telephone to call Dr. Reid. He had his home phone number and he just hoped that the professor was there to pick up.

Finally he heard a click. “Hello, this is Dr. Reid.”

“It’s Tex. Listen, I’ve only got a minute. I just want you to know that my compartment on the train was ransacked while I was in the dining car.”

“Did they take anything?” he asked sharply.

“Fortunately, no. I’ve got to get back onboard, but watch your back. I don’t know who did this or what they think they’re after, but if they know I met with you-”

“I understand completely,” Dr. Reid said. “I will be alright.”

“Good. I have to go.”

“Please call if you have other news.”

“I will.”

Tex hung up and got back on board the train, making his way swiftly to his compartment. He had chosen not to notify the conductor about the invasion. That would just lead to questions and heightened security which might scare off whoever it was. While he didn’t relish the thought of a confrontation, it might be the only way to figure out who was after him and why.

Once he had sealed himself inside and placed his gun within easy reach he opened up the packet of papers that

Dr. Reid had entrusted to him. The first thing he looked at was an actual clipping of the news article from the Arizona paper that the professor had referenced.

The article was quite lengthy and he read it slowly, trying to absorb as much of the detail as he could. It seemed that an explorer named Kincaid had discovered the cave after noticing some stairs cut into the wall of the canyon. He had shortly thereafter returned with a full team of Smithsonian scientists.

The cave system itself was described in detail. Inside were mummies, a shrine, and weapons of war. The cave system was so extensive that it was estimated that at one point 50,000 people could have lived there. It was all extraordinary and he made sure to note important details like the distance from the mouth of the cave to the first great chamber.

The more he read, though, the more nervous he became. If even a fraction of it were true finding the Tear in those caves would prove to be like finding a needle in a haystack. He wouldn't even begin to know where to look. What made matters worse was that there had been teams of people tromping through there disturbing things. How did he know that it wasn't sitting in some dusty storage room at the Smithsonian or in the trophy room of some researcher? He didn't. He was going in there in the hopes that everyone else had been too blind to find it. He had gone after artifacts on slim information before, but this was ludicrous. He was beginning to think he should have drug the professor along just for an extra pair of eyes. Maybe the cat would have walked right to it. After all, the animal often appeared to be almost psychic.

He set the article aside, knowing full well that he'd probably read it a couple more times just to make sure he had everything committed to memory. The next thing he found was a crude map of the Grand Canyon showing the Colorado river winding through it.

A second map showed up a close detail of one section of the river. On it there were handwritten notes and an X had been drawn at one spot. Clearly that was where Dr. Reid thought the cave was located.

The next piece of paper held some scribbled notes from the professor, mostly remarking on items in the article. Toward the bottom, though, something caught Tex's eye.

No mention of finding burial of a pharaoh or other ruler. Start search there.

He was right. They'd found mummies and what appeared to be a soldier's barracks, but there was no indication that the explorers had found any kind of royal burial.

The Tear on Kauai had been located on royal grounds, but it hadn't been connected to any kind of a burial. Nor was there anything special and ceremonial about where and how it was hidden. He wondered what made Dr. Reid think this one would be different.

No doubt there had been some obscure reference in some dusty tome that he had read ages ago. At this point the professor himself might not even remember what had led him down this particular path of thought.

Given that there wasn't reference to a royal burial, if one did it exist it might not have been found and contaminated by the investigative team. That was as good a reason as any to start his search off by looking for such a burial.

It was well after midnight when he finally put the papers all back in the envelope. He had hoped that whoever had searched his room would have shown up by now. He didn't relish the idea of going to sleep when he well knew he might wake up to an unwelcome visitor.

He couldn't spend the next three days in a constant state of wakefulness, though. There was a remote possibility that whoever it was had gotten off at the last stop when they were unable to locate whatever it was they were looking for. It was far more likely, though, that they were still aboard and would now be trying to find out what he was carrying on his person.

He thought of the woman from dinner, Lena. She had arrived in the dining car seconds after he had and he had left before her. There was no way she had time to search his room. It was possible, though, that she was just the distraction and she had an accomplice who was searching his room all the time she was flirting with him at dinner.

All the more reason to make sure he saw her at breakfast. Maybe she could answer a few questions for him. Of course that was if he survived until breakfast.

After preparing for bed he moved his luggage in front of the door, a tripping barrier for anyone trying to sneak in. Then he took the blankets and pillows off the bed and bunked down on the floor. Someone shooting through the door hoping to hit the bed would only kill the mattress that way and not him. Then, gun under his pillow, he settled down to sleep.

He awoke in the morning grateful to be alive and surprised that he had been able to pass the night in peace.

He got ready for the day being sure to once again have the papers and the Tear on him before he left his compartment.

He made his way to the dining car, intent on talking to Lena whenever she finally showed. He was surprised to find that she was already there. “Good morning,” he greeted her as he slid into the seat across from her.

“Good morning,” she said, not smiling quite as much as she had the night before.

“Everything alright?” he asked as he placed his napkin in his lap.

She nodded. “After dinner it turned out to be an uneventful evening. I turned in early.”

“Sounds boring,” he said.

“Did you have more excitement than I did?” she asked as she picked up a cup of tea and sipped from it.

“Oh, you know, the usual,” he said vaguely. He flagged down the waiter.

After ordering Tex turned back to Lena. “While last night’s dinner was certainly pleasurable, don’t you think it’s about time we talked business?”

“If we must,” she said, wrinkling up her nose in distaste.

“Oh, I think it’s past time,” Tex said. “So, what is it your boss wants from me?”

“He wants your help to find the spear,” she said with a sigh.

“The spear?” Tex asked. “Which spear would that be, exactly?”

“The only one worth having, of course. The Spear of Destiny.”

He stared at her in surprise. That was not anything like what he had expected her to say. "You mean the one that belonged to Longinus the centurion?"

"Yes, the spear that pierced the Christ's side."

He shook his head. "Lady, your boss is chasing after fairy tales. That spear would have been destroyed or lost nearly two millennia ago."

"And yet it was not," she said, still sounding bored by the conversation. "He has proof that it exists and clues as to where it is now."

It was a tantalizing thought. It was possible that the followers of Jesus had taken possession of the lance and hid it somewhere for safe keeping. It was possible that the centurion, who was supposedly moved by the entire experience, had done the same. The question was, where could you hide something that it would remain hidden for nearly two thousand years?

Maybe in a cave in the Grand Canyon, he thought drily.

"Why me? Why doesn't your boss just go after it himself?"

"He is unable to, and he chose you because you have a reputation as being an honest man as well as one who is not afraid to go after what he wants." She paused and stared at him for a moment with eyes that smoldered. "Are you the type of man who goes after what he wants?" she asked suggestively.

"When I see something I want, yes," he said, subtly insulting her.

She either didn't notice or didn't care. She continued on. "He's willing to pay a great deal of money."

"Of course he is. That's one of a kind, priceless."

"He's willing to pay you handsomely even if you ultimately can't find the spear."

That gave Tex pause. Few collectors were that generous. As a rule they paid for results, not effort.

"As tempting as the offer is, I'm afraid I'll have to decline," Tex said.

"Why? Has someone else already hired you to go after the spear? If so, we can offer you double what they are."

Things were getting interesting now. The waiter returned with coffee and set it down. Tex picked up his cup of coffee. "Why so much interest in the spear now after all this time?" he asked.

It was his way of implying that he was aware that there were other interested parties.

"I don't know," she said.

She was lying.

"Well, tell your boss I wish I could help, but I'm just a teacher. I wouldn't be any use in the field."

"He will be very disappointed to hear that," she said.

"Disappointed enough to ransack my compartment again?"

"I don't know what you're talking about," she said, dropping her eyes to the table.

"You're not a very good liar. What was it he was looking for while you kept me busy at dinner?"

"I don't know."

"You can do better than that."

"I told you, I don't know. He was probably hoping to find something he could use as blackmail, leverage, to get you to do what he wanted."

"And what exactly does he have on you?"

"Nothing," she said but the sudden red of her cheeks betrayed her.

"Tell you what. How about I make this really easy. You're going to take me to see him right now."

She looked up, her eyes wide in what appeared to be real fear. "No, you mustn't."

"Oh, trust me, I must," Tex said.

He stood and took her upper arm in his hand. He practically had to yank her to her feet. Fortunately at the last she came willingly. The last thing he needed at that moment was to make a scene in the dining car.

"Okay, take me to him," he said as soon as they had left the dining car behind.

She nodded, seemingly resigned. He let go of her arm and followed her through the train until they came to one of the compartments. "This one is his. Mine's next door," she said.

Her face was a study in misery and he couldn't help but wonder just what sort of monster he was about to come face-to-face with. He was also having problems keeping himself from speculating about what the hold Lena's boss had on her was.

He knocked on the door and waited a moment. There was no answer. He glanced at Lena. and then pulled his gun out of the shoulder holster that he was wearing under his jacket. He pushed on the door, and it opened easily revealing an empty room.

Lena started and stepped inside. "He was here! Last night he was here. Where did he go?"

"Looks like he got off the train early, and without you."

He had expected her to look relieved, but instead she just looked more worried.

"What's wrong? Liked him better than you cared to let on?" Tex asked as he holstered his gun and moved into the room. He began looking around to see if the man had left anything behind.

"No, it's just, he never does anything without a really good reason."

"And you're worried about what his good reason for leaving suddenly and without you was?"

She nodded.

"What's his name?"

"I don't know. He goes by so many, never the same one twice."

"Humor me. Let's hear some of them," he said.

She began to list a series of names. Once she had finished he shook his head in frustration. None of them meant anything to him.

"When did you last see him?"

"After dinner. He was frustrated that he hadn't found what he was looking for in your room."

"And that would be?"

"I told you, I don't know. He never tells me anything except what I need to know and last night I was supposed to keep you at dinner for at least an hour so that he could search your compartment."

"Which you did and he did and no one ended up happy about," Tex said grimly. "Well, your boss might have ditched you, but you're sticking with me until we get where we're going."

"Los Angeles?" she asked.

He shook his head. Her boss really did keep her in the dark.

"No, we'll be getting off a little before that," he said. "Too bad you don't really have family in Phoenix."

"That was just something he told me to say," she told him, confirming his earlier suspicions.

Tex couldn't find anything in the compartment. The man hadn't left anything behind. When he had finished searching he turned to Lena.

"Let's see your compartment?"

"Why?"

"To make sure he's not hiding out in there."

They went back into the hall and moments later were stepping into her compartment. The dress that she had been wearing the night before was hanging up and a suitcase with clothes spilling out of it was in the center of the room. There was no sign of anyone else having been in there.

Tex debated what to do. If the man really was looking for blackmail to use to force Tex into getting him the Spear of Destiny then there didn't seem to be any harm in letting the girl go and forgetting about the whole incident. If, on the other hand, that had just been another cover story and he was after the Tear or information relating to it, then she could still prove to be valuable.

He decided that at this point he couldn't afford to take any chances. He sized her up. "So, here's how it's going to be. You're not going to budge from this compartment unless it's to join me in the dining car for a meal. I will escort you to and from, and I will be checking on you at random intervals to make sure you're doing as you're told."

"What am I, your hostage?" she asked, lips beginning to tremble.

"Don't think of me as your warden. Think of me as your bodyguard. As long as you stick close to me, nothing bad will happen to you. Do you understand?"

She nodded, eyes wide.

"Okay. I'll be back here a little later to take you to lunch. If you try to leave the train, I will catch you."

"And?" she asked.

"And, I wouldn't advise it," he said, letting a menacing tone creep into his voice.

She bit her lower lip and then dropped her eyes. It was okay if she was a little afraid of him. The truth was, since her boss had left her behind he didn't think she was valuable as a hostage. Rather he was starting to worry that she might be expendable and he didn't want that on his conscience.

He headed back to his compartment, mind racing. He would give anything to know if Lena and her boss's sudden interest in him were connected to his quest. It made him uneasy that there was a man out there whose name and face he didn't know who wanted something from him.

He spent the next few hours going over the papers from Dr. Reid again, committing everything to memory in case they were lost or he had to destroy them to keep them from falling into the wrong hands.

When at last he was satisfied that he could remember enough of the detail if need be he got up and stretched. He was hungry since he'd had to leave the dining car before getting his breakfast. It was close enough to lunch time. He secured all the papers and then headed out for Lena's compartment.

Once there he knocked on the door. "Lena, lunch."

He heard rustling and then what sounded more like a struggle. “Lena?” he called, drawing his gun.

Suddenly he heard her scream.

Tex threw open the door and raced into Lena’s compartment. Suddenly something struck him hard on the back of the head and everything went black.

Chapter 7

Even though Tex had learned to expect the unexpected sometimes even he was shocked by what he found. That was the case when he came to and discovered Lena pointing a gun at his head. He winced. His head was still ringing.

"So, I take it you don't want to go to lunch?" he asked.

"Funny and sweet. How can a girl resist?"

"Apparently pretty easily," he said, gingerly touching the back of his head with his hand.

He could see his gun behind her on the bed along with the envelope containing all the papers from Dr. Reid.

"Where is it?" she asked.

"Where is what? I still have no idea what you and your boss are looking for."

"Don't play dumb with me," she warned.

"I wouldn't dream of it. You're the one with the gun."

"Where is the gemstone?"

He blinked. She was after the Tear, only clearly she didn't know what it was. She also hadn't found it wrapped in the handkerchief in his one pocket. He had decided the handkerchief was more discrete than its original kapa cloth covering, but he hadn't dreamed someone would actually miss it entirely. Clearly she couldn't have had time to search him that well. He must not have been out for as long as he thought.

"What gemstone?" he asked.

Her eyes narrowed in anger, and she cocked the gun in her hand.

"Okay, it's in my compartment."

"No, that idiot cabin boy I paid to search it might not be very imaginative, but he is thorough."

"Cabin boy?" Understanding dawned on him. "Your boss was never on this train. The cabin next to yours was always empty."

"There's a good boy, you're catching on," she said with a smirk.

"I should have known, redheads are always trouble."

"You'll find out just how much trouble if you don't give me the gemstone."

"I told you. It's in my compartment. I had it on me during dinner, but then once my compartment had been searched I figured it would be safer to hide it where the thief had already looked."

"Alright. We can go there together and you can get it. On your feet."

He stood gingerly. "Why does your boss want it so badly anyway?" he asked, fishing for information.

"I didn't ask, and he didn't say."

"You're comfortable with that kind of arrangement?" he asked.

She shrugged. "It works for us."

There was no way he would be able to get past her to his gun. And if he lunged for hers the odds that it would go off were uncomfortably high. He was going to have to play this out as long as he could hoping for a chance to turn the tables on her.

"So, that whole Spear of Destiny thing, that was just something to keep me talking while your hired help searched my things? Your boss had no interest in the Spear, did he?"

"Oh no, that was a legitimate offer."

Tex stared at her. "He makes me a business offer while at the same time stealing from me? That makes no sense. I mean, none whatsoever. He'd have to realize I could never trust him, and because of that he wouldn't be able to trust me."

"All I know is that he wanted two things. He wanted the gemstone and he wanted you out of the country."

Tex's brain was working overtime as he tried to puzzle that one out. Why would the man want him out of the country? Was it because he didn't want Tex going after the second Tear? But why? If he wanted him out of the way he could have just had him killed or otherwise incapacitated. No, there was something more here that he was missing, something that went deeper. He had to figure out what it was.

Maybe he could sway Lena to his side. She had certainly been flirtatious at dinner the night before, but that could easily have just been a ruse on her part. There was only one way to find out.

"I've got an idea," he said. "Why don't you and I both get out of the country? Together?"

"And live on what?" she asked, arching one eyebrow. "It's my understanding that professors don't get paid that much."

"Yeah," he said, "but grave robbers can get paid very well."

"I see, so now you're admitting to your extracurricular activities?"

"I figure you're not going to tell," he said, letting his voice drop slightly. He took a small step toward her and smiled at her.

"And here I thought it wasn't just my offer that you had no interest in last night," she said, eyes burning through him.

"I am naturally cautious, but you are a fascinating woman, and the things we could do together..." he said, daring to hope that he was arousing her interest.

"I don't think that's in the cards," she said, her voice a little breathier.

"Why? You're not actually romantically involved with your boss, are you?"

She laughed. "Me and the old man? That's hilarious."

At least he knew one thing. Her boss was a much older man. He took a step closer to her. One more and he'd have a chance at getting the gun away from her. "Well then, I don't see a problem."

She shook her head slightly. "Only problem is you."

"I don't understand."

"You see, the old man told me about you. He warned me that you wouldn't be swayed by any of my charms. Apparently you were in love once and she tore your heart into itty bitty little bits. Looking at you last night I knew that was true."

"You don't need to worry about her, there's nothing she can do to us," Tex said, hating the fact that he could hear the hitch in his voice. It made him furious that even just thinking about her still upset him this much.

Lena cocked her head to the side, studying him. “She’s dead, isn’t she? What happened?”

“She betrayed me, and I killed her,” he said softly.

“Now that, I wager, is a story worth hearing. Only not right now,” Lena said, taking a step back. “Don’t get me wrong, I’d love to dance with you, but not today. Now we’re going to go get that gemstone so we can both start to put all this unpleasantness behind us.”

He tried one last tactic. “Whatever he’s paying you, I can double it.”

“Ah, sugar, there’s just not enough money in the world for that. With her free hand she picked up a fur stole which she draped over the gun. It was just enough to obscure it from the casual onlooker but not enough to keep her from being able to shoot him whenever and wherever she chose.

He turned toward the door and raised his hands to shoulder level.

“No need to advertise. You can put your hands down. I know you don’t have any other weapons on you.”

He opened the door and felt her push the gun into the small of his back. That instantly dissuaded him from his half-formed plan of slamming the door and running. Lena was smart, he’d give her that.

And her boss knew an awful lot about him. He was reeling, still trying to work that one out. An old man with a lot of money and enough sense to hire someone like her. An old man with a lot of money who wanted him out of the country and wanted the Tear.

“I’d love to meet your boss,” he said as he walked slowly in the direction of his compartment. Once they reached it he would be out of options so he planned on taking his time getting there.

"I wouldn't count on that," she said.

"This job of his, recovering the Spear of Destiny, would I be working with you?"

"You'd be communicating with me, that's for sure."

"But how about on location, in the field...exotic cities...potential danger at every turn. We'd be working together quite closely. I believe I would find that to be a tempting offer."

"As stimulating as that would be, you yourself have already pointed out the obvious problems with that," she said.

"I might have been a bit hasty."

"If he wants to offer you the job again, he will. Until then let's keep things simple, shall we?"

"Oh, but why do that when complicated is so much more fun?"

"If I believed even half of what you were spouting out of those pretty lips we might have something to talk about. Now, keep moving," she said, nudging him with the gun.

He had managed to slow nearly to a standstill and reluctantly he picked up his pace again. They were nearing his compartment and so far there hadn't been a single thing he could use as a diversion while he either made a run for it or tried to wrestle the gun from her. She must be concerned as well because she nudged him again with the gun.

"No tricks," she said.

"I will agree to a lot of things," he said, "but that certainly isn't one of them."

"I knew I liked you."

They were just two doors away from his compartment and desperation was starting to take hold. The train slowed suddenly and Tex took advantage of the moment. He dropped to the floor and kicked out at Lena. She fell with a cry and the gun started to topple from her hand. He snatched it up before it hit the floor and quickly turned it on her as he scrambled to his feet.

"You kicked me," she said, glaring up at him.

"Well you hit me so let's consider ourselves even," he said. "Now, into my compartment."

She slowly got up, bracing herself against the wall. Then she limped the few feet to his door. She opened it and he followed her inside, closing the door behind them.

"Sit," he said, indicating the bed.

She hobbled over and sat. "I'm going to need ice for the swelling," she said.

"Well, I need it for my head, but I figure if I can wait so can you."

"What do you want?" she asked.

"I want to know about your boss and why he wants the gemstone so badly."

The train was slowing way down, clearly nearing a stop.

"I told you, I don't know why he wants it," she said, glaring up at him.

"Not good enough."

"What do you want me to do? Make up something? Okay, maybe he likes big, purple rocks." Her voice was exasperated and she was clutching her ankle.

The train came to a stop at last and he could see people milling about at the station.

"What are you going to do with me? Lena asked, changing the subject.

"A lot of that depends on you and how cooperative you're feeling," he said. "Who knows, maybe your boss will be sending me a gemstone to ransom you."

"Don't count on it," she said in a dangerous voice.

"Not worth that much to him?"

"No, it's just-" her eyes went suddenly wide and she gasped. She was staring out the window.

"Who's out there?" he asked, risking a quick glance and not picking out anyone he knew.

"He wasn't supposed to meet me until the next station," she said.

Tex turned toward the window, eyes locking on the men outside. "Which one is-"

She leaped up, grabbed his head and slammed it into the window. Then she busted out of the door. Reeling from two head injuries now he tried to recover his sense of balance as he made his way after her.

He raced down the length of the one car, chasing after a bit of her skirt that he kept seeing disappear as she raced from one car to the next.

He made it to the last one just as the train lurched forward again. He saw her on the stairs. She blew him a kiss and then jumped onto the platform. Before he could move the train picked up more speed and she waved as he passed her.

He had messed up. He knew that. Perhaps subconsciously he had wanted her to escape. The truth was that trying to hold her hostage would have proven nearly impossible and the odds were high they would have switched places again with him once again at her mercy.

He went to her cabin, retrieved his papers and gun, and searched through her things. Unfortunately he couldn't come up with so much as a shred of information about her let alone any clues as to the identity of her employer. With a sigh he headed to the dining car where he ate a hasty lunch and then returned to his room.

Once there he retrieved his journal and a pen from his satchel. Then he sat down on the bed and prepared to document the events of the past twenty-four hours. When he had finished and skimmed it back over he found that he had written down more questions than facts.

Who is Lena's boss? had been written in several places. The question that appeared even more frequently was *How does Lena's boss know about the Tear?* It was safe in his possession for now. Unless he had agents waiting down the line that would board the train at a phone call from him or Lena then he should be safe for a while. Once he got to Arizona that might change, but for a few moments he could let his guard down enough to get some rest. He'd be grateful to be able to sleep on the bed tonight instead of on the floor.

Once he had finished with his journal he got ready for bed. He was looking forward to a better night's sleep now that he was reasonably certain no one would be trying to break into his room later that night.

The moment his head hit the pillow, though, he was consumed with thoughts of *her*. Lena had been right. He'd been in love once and had his heart torn to pieces. Jeanette had been her name. He had met her in graduate school. She was fun, smart, and highly competitive. He had loved her desperately. And deep down he still did even though he loathed himself for it.

The rest of the train ride was mercifully uneventful. He was able to get more rest and he tried using his left arm more and more when he could. He didn't like going into potentially dangerous situations when he wasn't functioning at his peak, but he had little choice. There had been an uncomfortable scratching in the back of his mind that told him that he didn't have as much time as he might think.

Within twenty-four hours after his arrival at his destination in Arizona he had done two things. First he had gone to a doctor and had the cast removed. He had always been a very fast healer and he was able to convince the man that he'd had the cast on for much longer than he actually had. Second he had begun the search for a guide to take him down the section of river he wanted to go. The second task was proving much harder to accomplish than the first.

It didn't help that the area he wanted to travel to was technically off-limits, something he was told in no uncertain terms by the first guide he approached. The second politely refused the job saying that he handled tourists, mostly families. He did suggest that Tex might do better with an Indian guide, someone whose family was native to the lands in question. While that seemed like a great piece of advice he found that he couldn't even get those guides to talk to him at all.

It had been Tex's experience that everywhere in the world money talked and people listened. There was somcthing else going on here, though, that was far more powerful than money. He finally figured out that it was superstition. Apparently the area of the canyon he wanted to go to was renowned for some sort of dark spirits that dwelled in the rocks.

He finally found one man who told him that the only one who might take him down that stretch of the river was a native named Hank. Apparently Hank was to be found that day at an outpost that was half grocery and half watering hole. It was the place to do business, though, especially if you didn't want other people nosing into that business.

Tex showed up in the late afternoon. The establishment seemed to be split down the middle, general store on the left side of the building and bar on the right. A couple of guys in the bar section were finishing a game of darts. The winner headed for a seat at the bar and the loser wondered into the store.

At the bar was a man that from his description had to be Hank. He was about six foot four with powerful shoulders and a long, thick braid of black hair that hung down nearly to his waist. He was wearing a knife on his belt.

The seat next to him was open and on the counter there was a small basket of apples, a little bleed over from the grocery. Tex walked up and sat down. "I'm looking for a guide to take me to this section of the canyon," he said, setting the rough map drawing he had down on the bar. "I was told I should speak to you."

The big man turned his head slightly and looked at the map. A moment later in one motion he unsheathed his knife and slammed it down into the bar within an inch of Tex's hand.

Chapter 8

"Is there a problem?" Tex asked carefully.

"Any man who wants to go there is crazy. The place is haunted. Bad spirits."

Tex had been called crazy too many times to let it faze him. What intrigued him was that the big man was the first one who would even acknowledge that he knew where Tex wanted to go.

"I need to go there. It is important. I will talk to the spirits and tell them that you are a good man and that any harm should only befall me."

The man narrowed his eyes in disdain. "White men who say they talk to spirits are liars."

"Just because I don't believe doesn't mean I don't respect," Tex said.

The other man continued sizing him up. "You wear a knife. Do you know how to use it?"

Tex nodded.

"Are you a warrior?"

"No."

"But you have killed others."

It was a statement, not a question. Tex did not bother to answer, just continued to gaze steadily at the other man.

"If I take you, I will not protect you."

"Nor would I expect you to. I can protect myself."

"Prove it."

"How?" Tex asked.

The big man pulled the knife out of the bar. He turned and hurled the knife. It hit the bullseye on a dart board hanging on the far wall. He walked over, retrieved it, and came back to his seat.

Tex stood and unsheathed his knife. He grabbed an apple from the basket on the bar. He felt the weight of it in his hand a moment. Then he tossed the apple in the air. A second later he threw the knife with enough force that it impaled the falling apple and carried it forward, pinning it to the dart board.

He walked over retrieved the knife and the apple and took a bite out of the latter. He walked back and sat down. All around them noise had stopped and all eyes were turned their way.

"It was a little right of center," the other man said.

Tex smiled. "So it was. But, then again, so is a man's heart when you're aiming for him."

The man nodded. "I am called Hank."

"Good to meet you, Hank. I'm Tex. Now, when can we leave?"

Two days later they were on the river and by Tex's calculations they had to be close to their destination. Even as he helped paddle he kept anxiously scanning the rock face for signs of the staircase that was supposedly cut into it.

They had been on the river since dawn and his right arm was aching since he was still using his left as sparingly as possible. At noon they'd had some jerky and water, but had stayed on the river, letting the current carry them for the most part, as they ate.

The sun was beating down hot on them, and he wished he had brought a swimsuit as he could use a dip in the water to cool off. As it was he was wearing his standard gear for whenever he was in the field. He had the sleeves of his khaki shirt rolled up to his elbows and wished he could likewise roll up the legs of his khaki pants. Both shirt and pants were replete with pockets and rings to hang things off of. It was the kind of gear preferred by archaeologists and big game hunters alike. He wore a red bandana around his neck that he could use to cover his nose and mouth when needed. As usual he was wearing his gun belt which also had a scabbard attached for his knife. The Colt 45 rested in its holster. His other gun and his shoulder holster he had stowed in his satchel for the time being. You never could tell what you'd need in the field. Both his brown leather hiking boots and brown leather satchel were scuffed and worn, survivors of many encounters with the unknown. His hat, also a dark brown, was brand new. It seemed he never could keep a hat more than a couple of weeks. He usually never even had time to break one in properly before it was lost or destroyed.

Tex had lost track of just how many places he'd been and how many wonders he'd seen. This venture, however, was Tex's first time to the Grand Canyon and the beauty and size of it took his breath away. He felt that it was vast enough to easily conceal a lost civilization inside cliff caves. Even as he admired its size and grandeur, though, it also made his task seem more daunting.

His guide was quite knowledgeable, but not the talkative kind. That was fine with Tex who was busy wondering what he was going to find, if anything. He kept hoping this whole thing wasn't a wild goose chase. Sitting in a library in Washington D.C. discussing an ancient Egyptian civilization hidden in the Grand Canyon was one thing. Actually being here actively looking for it was quite another.

Oftentimes it seemed the only thing that separated the brilliant discoverers and explorers from crazy fools was the amount of luck on their side. Heinrich Schliemann had been a crazy fool wandering around with a copy of the *Iliad* clutched in his fist and babbling about Troy until he stuck a shovel in the earth and actually found it.

Tex just hoped that in this particular adventure he would be as fortunate as Heinrich had been. The more he stared at the walls of the canyon, though, the less optimistic he felt.

Suddenly Hank turned the canoe into the shore.

"What's wrong?" Tex asked.

"This is as far as I will take you."

"I don't see what I'm looking for."

Hank jumped out of the canoe when they ran aground and reluctantly Tex did the same. Together they drug it up onto the shore.

"I know what you are looking for. You're seeking the cursed cave. What you're seeking is less than a quarter of a mile from here."

Tex wasn't entirely surprised that Hank had guessed his intention based off the description he'd given him of the area he wanted to go and the staircase he was looking for.

"Have you seen the cave?"

"No."

"But you know we're close?"

“Yes.”

“Why not drop me off closer?” Tex asked.

Hank shook his head. “I will not wait on the shore that close.”

Whatever Hank thought the cave was haunted by it certainly had him spooked. Tex knew better than to persuade him otherwise about the cave. The things a man believed deeply were rarely changed by arguments from any other man, let alone a stranger.

“But you will wait here for me, right?” Tex said, seeking reassurance of that much.

Hank’s face betrayed his uneasiness and Tex realized he might have a problem on his hands, especially since they had only one canoe. “I’m paying you to wait for me, not drop me off and leave me for dead,” he pressed.

“I will wait two hours.”

“Ten hours,” Tex haggled.

“Four.”

“Eight.”

Hank sighed, looking supremely uneasy. “I will wait no more than five. We must be away from this place before nightfall. I wait five hours, not one minute longer, and then I leave.

“Okay,” Tex agreed. He wasn’t happy. It could take him easily an hour or more just to find the cave and get up to it. If it was as vast inside as the article seemed to indicate he’d barely have a chance to scrape the surface before he’d have to hurry back. He couldn’t do anything about it, though, but hope that Hank would actually stay the full five hours. “Five hours. I’ll be here.”

Hank nodded and turned to tend to the canoe. Tex grabbed his satchel out of it which contained, among other things, a flashlight. He slung it over his body and then set out at a fast walk hoping that the stairs wouldn't be hard to find.

As it was, a few minutes later, he nearly missed them. He had drawn parallel with them when he noticed a sudden discoloration of the wall that seemed out of place. When he stepped closer to the rock wall he realized that high above his head there were indeed stairs. Some walking and a bit of climbing would be required to get to them, though. He couldn't see a cave from where he was standing, but had to trust that one was up there.

Mindful to protect his left arm when he could he started up. It was agonizingly slow going and several times he had sharp pain in his left arm. Regardless of whether or not the bone was healed all the way the muscles had atrophied a lot in the time he'd been confined to the cast and twisting hurt. When he made it to the stairs it was a relief, but he still had to be cautious because of how narrow they were.

At last he mounted a ledge and saw the mouth of a cave which the ledge had hidden from his view when he was below. He felt a tingle of excitement as he usually did when he was on the precipice of discovery. The stairs were here as was the cave. Would he actually find remnants of Egyptian civilization inside?

He glanced back up the river and could make out the canoe on the shore. At least Hank hadn't already left him. That was some small consolation. Still, he needed to be mindful of the time.

Tex got out his flashlight and shone it inside, inspecting the structure itself. One wall looked natural, eroded by water and time while the other had several sections that had distinctive markings on them that looked to be placed there by some sort of tool. It was likely that the cave entrance had been widened slightly or at least had protruding bits of rock removed.

He shone the flashlight down on the ground, looking for any holes or signs of unfriendly animals. The floor itself appeared solid enough and was clean of any sort of imprints. If any human or animal had been inside the cave it had been a long time ago.

He stepped carefully forward, testing the ground with his feet before trusting his weight fully to it. He walked forward a dozen steps and then stopped again, lifting his head and swinging the flashlight around once more. Both walls now were covered with markings left by tools.

The newspaper article had reported that the crypt with the mummies was several hundred feet inside this main shaft. With the time he had before his guide would abandon him he couldn't afford to tarry. Taking a deep breath he pushed forward, keeping the flashlight sweeping from walls to cave floor as he tried to get a better grasp of the tunnel he was moving through and make sure he didn't trip over anything.

Several feet in the cave branched out on both sides. He could feel his curiosity burning within him. Was it true that this whole place was a massive cave system? The article had said that the original explorer claimed that 50,000 could live in here. It seemed too impossible to be true. It all did.

However, as impossible as it would be, he needed it to be true. If it wasn't then his search to understand the mysterious gem he'd found would be over before it was hardly begun.

He kept moving, picking up speed as he grew more comfortable in the darkness. Silence had descended. He couldn't hear anything from the outside world and only his own footfalls echoed in this inner world. He had no idea how far he had traveled and he cursed his own negligence in not counting his steps. It was an amateur mistake.

He paused when his light revealed tunnels going off on either side. He shone his light down first one then the other but it didn't penetrate the darkness very far. He pressed on. If the article was to be believed then those tunnels indicated that he was a little over halfway to the large room he was looking for. He kept going, counting his steps now.

He sensed the room before he could actually see it. A change in the air, a feeling of space instead of confinement. Then, a moment, later he swung his flashlight in a slow arc and could not find the walls of the tunnel. From here on out he would have to be especially cautious, aware of his exact location if he ever hoped to make it back out alive let alone in time to meet up with his guide.

It was a good sign, this larger space right where it should be. Of course, it was possible that the description of the cave itself had been accurate while the description of the fantastic contents had been a hoax.

Even if it hadn't been a hoax there was the possibility that everything had long ago been carted off by the Smithsonian or other adventurers or archaeologists. Of course, that scenario begged the question of how it had been kept such a secret, and the even more pressing question of why it had been kept a secret.

He turned around and played his flashlight down the tunnel he had just come from. Then he moved it slightly to the side and saw the wall of the chamber in which he was now standing. He moved the light to his left, following the wall. Relief washed over him as his flashlight picked out what appeared to be a torch laying at the base of the wall. He moved toward it and picked it up. From his pouch he drew a piece of cloth which he wrapped around the charred remains of the one on the torch. He tipped a small vial of oil over it next before pulling out his lighter and setting the torch ablaze.

With its light to allow him to explore he was able to place the flashlight in the center of the entrance to the room so he could easily find his way back to the tunnel that led out of the cave system. With that taken care of, he held the torch aloft and moved toward what should be the center of the room.

A few steps in he caught a reflection as of light bouncing off metal. It was coming from his right. He turned his steps in that direction and seconds later was rewarded.

At his feet was an armored breastplate, as one would wear into battle. He knelt beside it and brought his torch down for a closer look. It appeared to be made of copper. There was layers of dust and grime on it, but he could still see the shine of the light in the metal. It didn't look like it had been sitting there for centuries. Rather it looked like it hadn't been disturbed in a couple of decades. That would fit with the timeframe for the research team that had supposedly visited this place.

He stood and took a couple of more steps as his light reflected off more items. A couple of feet away he found a neat stack of spears. He touched an edge and discovered they were still quite sharp.

He was fascinated and he found himself wanting to examine each item more closely. He had to sternly remind himself that he didn't have time for that, though. He needed to follow Dr. Reid's written suggestion and look for a royal burial.

Regretfully he turned aside and retraced his steps. When he was once again parallel to the tunnel leading to the outside world, he turned and continued his trek straight across the center of the chamber.

He walked another thirty feet, wondering when he was going to finally make it to the other side. He turned, making sure he could still make out the light from the flashlight. If he lost sight of that he'd be in serious danger.

He could still see the pinpoint of light in the darkness. He turned back, intent to continue across the chamber.

He had taken a dozen more steps when he stopped, heart pounding as he stared at the figure before him.

Chapter 9

Tex took a deep breath as he realized that he was staring at a giant idol, sitting with legs crossed and holding a flower in each hand. The stone it was made from gleamed like marble in the flickering torch light. As he stepped forward he could make out other figures surrounding the idol. The newspaper article had speculated that this was a religious figure, maybe even an image of Buddha, and he could definitely see why that would have sprung instantly to mind for those exploring the cave system. The truth was it might have been given the way it looked. Although that didn't match with the supposed Egyptian findings throughout the rest of the cave. Perhaps it represented two different periods of occupation by two different groups. That didn't feel right, though.

Something stirred in the back of his mind. He had seen something like this image before, on a tablet. He strained, trying to remember where it had been. It finally came to him with a rush. It had been in Dr. Reid's office when Tex was still one of his students. The professor had indicated that the strange tablet was Egyptian in origin, but Tex had only had a glance at it and found none of the figures familiar.

As usual Dr. Reid knew more than what he was telling. Tex had to wonder for just a moment if he was on this treasure hunt for himself as he had originally thought or if he had been manipulated into it by his former mentor.

The newspaper article had also indicated that somewhere nearby would be the crypt where the mummies were. They were stacked in such a way to almost seem as though it were a barracks. They wouldn't have what he was looking for, though. For a prize such as he was after he'd have to find a pharaoh, or the equivalent, buried in here. That was the conclusion Dr. Reid had drawn and Tex wasn't going to argue with it.

A royal burial was something that had not been mentioned in the newspaper article and whether the mysterious research team had found anything like that could only be speculated at.

What did seem unlikely is that such a high ranking member of the society would be laid to rest in one of the open chambers. More likely it would have been sealed in some way. He stepped quickly around the idol and made his way to the far wall. He walked along it, working his way around the room clockwise.

In here in the darkness he realized he had lost all sense of time. He didn't even know how much he had left before his guide would leave him stranded. That knowledge caused him to move faster.

When he came across the entrance to the barracks chamber he only stepped briefly inside, long enough to confirm that it was as had been described. There were rows of mummies settled into niches in the stones three high, like some macabre bunk beds. Every wall was covered with them except for the space in the door. He doubted that another chamber led from there.

He returned to the large chamber and continued his circumnavigation. He found more artifacts, but he refused to stop and take a good look at them since he had a clock ticking in his head that was causing him to grow more and more agitated. He came across another tunnel, and he shone the torch down it and walked a handful of feet. Finally he shook his head in frustration as he returned to the large chamber.

He didn't have time to explore the side tunnels either here or closer to the cave entrance. He might have to give up and come back although he wasn't sure he'd be able to persuade Hank to bring him back again.

Back in the large room he kept walking until he stepped over his flashlight and moved on to the left side of the chamber. He kept going, hoping he would find something.

When he came to the next wall he was almost all the way down it before he realized that there was nothing there. No openings, no passageways, no artifacts, just a bare wall met his questing eyes.

He turned and slowly retraced his steps until he was standing roughly at the middle of the wall. The stone had been swept smooth. There were no outcroppings of rock nor were there any markings of any kind. He lifted the torch high and examined the wall closely searching for anything that seemed out of place. At last he found a slight indentation roughly five feet off the ground. It was shallow and not very long. If it hadn't been for the extreme smoothness of the stone around it he wouldn't even have noticed it. It was roughly the size of one of his fingernails.

He pressed the tip of his finger into it, but the rock didn't give. He pressed harder, but still there was nothing.

He felt his frustration mounting. Time was slipping away and he needed to find that Tear.

He blinked as a thought came to him. The indentation in the rock was roughly the same shape and size as the Tear he had already discovered. On a hunch he unzipped the pocket on the inside of his jacket where he kept the first Tear. He pulled out the piece of cloth it was wrapped in and quickly freed it. He pressed it into the indentation of the rock and it fit.

He moved his hand away as the Tear began to heat up. Even though he stopped touching it, the Tear's dark hue continued to change and at last the stone glowed red. He didn't know what it was reacting to since the only thing he knew of that activated it was living tissue. He waited, wondering if anything else was going to happen.

He stood for a full minute before shaking his head in frustration. He didn't know what he had been expecting, but other than the gem reacting nothing had happened. He reached out, intent on removing it from the wall when all of a sudden he saw something shimmer into existence.

Where once there had been a blank wall around the indentation writing began to appear. It was hieroglyphics. He touched the wall and found that it was suddenly hot. Somehow the Tear must have heated the stone and the writing must only show up when that was the case. The heat from his torch hadn't revealed the secret writing and the indentation was made for a Tear. Whoever had constructed this wall and left the writing had meant for it only to be read by someone already in possession of one of the Tears. It would have been impossible to find without it. Which meant that this was something the researchers never would have seen.

The thrill of discovery thrummed through his veins as he took out a notebook and hastily began to translate the words he was seeing. He had a feeling he'd be wanting to study the exact meaning of it all later.

When he came to the last symbol he paused. It wasn't Egyptian. Instead it was five ovals arranged in a lopsided half circle with the left side lower than the right. Squiggly lines appeared inside each oval. He had never seen any symbol like it before.

He put away his notebook and pencil and leaned closer to the symbol. It was the key, it had to be since it was different from everything else. Suddenly it clicked. The five ovals represented fingerprints, hence the lines inside each one. He held up his hand and placed his fingers on the circles and pushed.

With a groan the whole section of the wall moved inward. He kept pressing until it stopped. The section of wall was now sitting nearly two feet back from the rest. He debated for a moment whether to remove the Tear, but decided to leave it where it was in case it was still interacting with the wall in some way. He didn't want to lose the Tear but he also didn't want to find himself suddenly sealed inside a tomb with no way out.

He moved around the wall to the right and once he had cleared it he lifted his torch high to illuminate the hidden chamber. The dancing flames reflected off hundreds of gold items ranging from small jars to a full-size chariot. Gemstones of all colors danced and winked in the light.

Everything someone would possibly want in the afterlife was represented in some way. Food, transportation, it was all there at least in a representative sense. He saw several jars filled with what looked to be preserved human organs. Awestruck he made his way slowly deeper into the chamber until at last he was staring at a sarcophagus. Strangely, it was one of the few things in the room not made of gold. It was simple stonework, though the etchings on it were elaborate. He regretted that he was running out of time and couldn't copy those down in his notebook as well.

Whoever had constructed the wall to hide this burial understood the power and the nature of the Tears, probably far more than Tex did. If there was a Tear in this room they would have known its value. They would have buried it with the pharaoh himself.

Tex pulled a small crowbar from his satchel, praying it and he were strong enough for the task. He found a place to wedge it just underneath the lid of the sarcophagus. He threw his weight into it, trying to shift the lid, but it wouldn't budge.

He renewed his efforts, straining. Pain radiated up his left arm. The metal of the crowbar groaned in his hands and began to cut into them. With a curse he finally let go. There was no way he was going to be able to move the lid. If the Tear had been buried with the pharaoh it was lost to him. Even if he could convince his guide to bring him here one more time he didn't know what he could do to move such an unwieldy stone short of dynamiting it which would surely destroy everything within.

In Egypt they buried their pharaohs in such a manner as to try and keep everyone out. He had believed just for a moment that the fact that the ancients who had built this place had left a way in meant that they wanted someone to be able to find the Tear. Maybe that wasn't the case. If they didn't want anyone finding it, though, why leave a way into the burial chamber at all?

He began to examine the massive stone lid more carefully. His eyes moving across its surface. Finally he saw something that looked familiar. It was an indentation similar to the one on the wall outside. Could it be possible that the answer to one was also the answer to the other?

He walked back to the entrance to the chamber, his heart beginning to pound. What if he was wrong and this was a trap? It was a chance he was just going to have to take.

He moved around the wall. He took a deep breath and pried the Tear loose, wincing as it burned his fingers. He managed to drop it in his pocket before it burned too deeply.

Suddenly the wall began to close, just as he had feared. He grabbed it with his hand, but there was no stopping it. He had a split-second to make a choice that would change his life or possibly end it. Gritting his teeth he squeezed into the chamber.

As the wall closed completely with a thud a shiver danced up his spine. He was gambling that those who built this place wanted him to find the Tear and escape with it. If he was wrong then he was dead.

The torch was beginning to burn low as he hurried back to the sarcophagus. He fished the still warm Tear out of his pocket and placed it in the indentation he had found while holding his breath.

The Tear began to turn fiery red like it had outside. He waited. Five seconds. Ten. Twenty.

Panic was beginning to set in when at last he could see the shimmering as something that had been invisible suddenly became visible. This time there were no hieroglyphs, just the five ovals in a half circle. They were located in the center of the massive lid.

He placed his fingers on the circles and then slowly twisted them counter-clockwise. There was a groan and a moment later the stone slab began to rotate, moved only by the motion of his hand. He moved toward the head of the sarcophagus as the bottom of the slab swung toward him. When it had reached a ninety degree angle to the sarcophagus it came to a stop and wouldn't budge any further.

He held his torch so he could look down inside. A mummy lay, preserved for eternity. On its head it wore a golden death mask. As he bent closer he felt his breath catch in his throat. Beneath the left eye was a tear-shaped gem of purple-black that looked familiar. The second Tear!

He pried it up with his fingernail and quickly wrapped it in cloth even as it heated up. He placed it in his inside pocket before repositioning his fingers on the cover and returning the stone to its resting place. He pulled up his original Tear and tucked it inside his pocket as well.

He quickly headed toward the stone wall, praying that there was a way to get out and that he hadn't just doomed himself to share the pharaoh's grave. He reached the wall with the torch flickering out. He didn't have more cloth for the torch and would have to start burning his clothes for light if he didn't get out of there soon. In the fading light he frantically began running his free hand over the wall, trying to see if there was an indentation for one of the Tears as there had been on the other side.

He couldn't see anything and as he could feel himself starting to panic his torch sputtered and went out plunging him into complete darkness. He dropped the dead torch at his feet. Free to use both hands now he felt along the wall in a darkness so complete that it hurt his straining eyes. Fear was mounting in him. He didn't want to die, and to go out in this manner, with no one knowing what had happened to him was his worst nightmare. He thought of Dr. Reid. He alone would suspect what had happened to Tex. Would he come looking for him, though?

Tex very much doubted it. On the remote chance that the professor did, he would never find him without the help of a Tear to open the wall. Even if that hadn't been an issue he would arrive far too late to save Tex from suffocation or starvation, both of which seemed like terrifying ways to die.

He pulled a Tear out of his pocket and placed it against the stone, hoping that the contact would trigger something to happen, even if the stone wasn't in the right place. The stone began to heat up, soon glowing red hot. By its light he searched but still couldn't find anything. The stone wasn't reacting at all.

With a sharp hiss of pain he dropped the Tear as it burned the fingers on his left hand. It hit the ground and the red glow faded. He quickly bent down and scooped it up, returning it to his pocket. If he did manage to get out of here he didn't want to have to leave it behind because he couldn't see where he'd dropped it.

At last his right hand found what appeared to be an indentation in the wall, and he gasped with relief. With his left hand he reached into his pocket and removed the first Tear and pressed it into place. It began to slowly glow red, the light very dim but a relief to Tex's straining eyes. He waited impatiently for ovals to light up on the wall showing him where to put his fingers.

The Tear glowed brighter and brighter and then finally seemed to peak. He counted in his head, and when sixty seconds had passed he felt himself beginning to panic again. In both other places the oval markings had shown up by now. Was it possible he had put the Tear in the wrong place?

He moved his hands again over the rock, feeling for any other indentation. After a couple of minutes he finally found one not that far from the first. He started to remove the Tear to transfer it, but thought better of it at the last moment. He removed the second Tear from his pocket and instead pressed it into the second indentation.

The affect was instantaneous. The second Tear began to glow and the first Tear waxed brighter in intensity. Within seconds the ovals he had been looking for began appearing. This time, though, there were ten of them instead of five. He carefully positioned both hands and then pressed. The wall gave slightly then stopped. He released the pressure and it moved back closer to him, and he could feel a slight rush of air coming from the sides of the section. He moved a couple of steps to the side and was able to hook his fingers into a minor gap between the two sections of wall and pull the moveable one back into the chamber to where it had rested when it first opened.

When it had opened as far as it could, he snatched both Tears from their resting places and scooted through the already closing opening into the main chamber. The wall slid shut behind him with a thud.

His dead torch was inside the sealed room, but his flashlight was still shining on the floor near the tunnel that would lead to the exit. He wrapped both Tears separately in the cloth he had carried the first one in and stuffed them in his inner pocket. The fingers on his left hand were scalded. He would have to worry about that later. It was time to get out of here before he had to find his own way back to civilization.

He moved quickly toward the flashlight. He had lost all track of how much time he had been gone from his guide. The Grand Canyon covered well over a million acres of land and there was more than 250 miles of the Colorado River that ran through it. It was his first trip to the area and he knew that he couldn't find his way back if he had to. Just following the river out wasn't an option either with no food or other supplies.

Fortunately the journey back out of the cave took far less time than the journey in. When he reached the ledge just outside the mouth of the cave he took the stairs down as far as they went. He then climbed and slid the rest of the way down to the river bank.

Once on the ground he started walking as quickly as he could on the rough terrain as he headed for where he had left his guide. When the canoe came in sight he breathed a sigh of relief. Hank was sitting next to the boat, his back against a rock, staring at the water.

"I'm glad to see you here," Tex said as he walked up behind him.

His guide didn't acknowledge him in any way.

"Time to get going."

The man still didn't move or speak. The hair on the back of Tex's neck stood up. Reacting on instinct he dropped into a crouch, half expecting to hear the report of a rifle and have a bullet go whizzing over his head.

All was silent, though, except for the sound of the river. After a moment he crept forward until he could get a look at the man's face. Hank was dead.

Chapter 10

Hank was staring at the river, but with eyes that would see no more. Tex didn't need to check the man's pulse. His face had already taken on the grayish pallor of death. What had killed him was far more of a puzzle. There was no obvious signs of injury and no blood on the body at all that he could see.

There was a canteen of water next to him, one that neither of them had drank from earlier. Was it possible he was poisoned or could this be natural causes with really terrible timing?

"Just once why can't something go according to plan?" Tex muttered.

He glanced around uneasily. If the man had somehow been murdered his killer could be nearby. One more reason to get out of there fast. He studied the river for a moment. They had gotten here by paddling downstream. The current was too strong to fight so returning by canoe the way he had come would be impossible. That meant he could either take his chances and continue down the river, hoping to find a place to leave the canyon, or he could hike back toward where they had entered the river. The journey had to be a good twelve miles at least and over uneven terrain and at least one stretch had banks so steep he would have to wade through the water fighting the current. Night would most certainly fall before he could make it back and he would have to camp near the river overnight. Either way he could easily find himself in a lot of trouble. And that was if no one was trying to kill him.

He grabbed the canoe and shoved it into the water. His guide had wanted him back by this time so that they could get out of the canyon by nightfall. That meant that somewhere down the way there had to be a good place to exit. He just hoped he could find it. He jumped in, grabbed a paddle and pushed off from shore.

He had no time to bury the man and couldn't afford the questions that would be asked if he took the body with him. Maybe someone else would come along soon and take care of the body before the buzzards would save everyone the trouble. He couldn't help but shiver as the thought crossed his mind that maybe the ghosts the man was so afraid of had come to claim him and make him one of them.

He paddled hard for fifteen minutes until his injured arm couldn't take much more. The current picked up slightly and he used the paddle sparingly just to keep the boat in the center of the river. He kept a sharp lookout for anything that looked like it could be a path in the mountain up to the rim. He also looked over his shoulder frequently, but he could see no one following him.

He thought back over what he had read in the newspaper article. Where the cave was should be a little more than 40 miles upriver from the El Tovar hotel on the south rim of the canyon. At the speed at which he was traveling that was about ten hours away. No way he'd make it there before sunset. He couldn't risk floating past it in the dark so unless he saw something that looked like a way out before that then he'd be stopping to camp after all.

A few hours later Tex pulled the canoe up on the shore in the fading light. He decided against building a fire since he didn't want to attract visitors be they human or animal. He ate some beef jerky he had in his satchel and then curled up on the floor of the canoe between the seats and tried to get some sleep.

He had just drifted off when he heard something, almost like a splash in the water, that snapped him awake. He lay very still, straining his ears. There was another soft splashing sound and then a step. He tensed and slowly moved his hand to the hilt of the knife that he carried in a sheath in the back of his waistband.

Another soft step as he eased the knife out and moved his arm so he had the knife flat against his chest. Moments later a dark figure loomed over him. Tex caught the glint of moonlight on metal and realized the other man had a knife as well.

Tex leaped up, swiping with his own weapon and slashed the man across the chest. The man howled in pain and jabbed at Tex with his knife. He barely managed to jump back out of the way in time, but tripped and fell backward into the canoe, cracking his head hard on one of the seats.

He grunted and struggled to maintain consciousness. The man lumbered toward him again, and Tex kicked out with his feet as hard as he could. The man fell, and Tex struggled to get up and out of the canoe. The other man was trying to get up as well, and Tex kicked him.

"Who are you?" he demanded.

The man didn't say anything, but out of the corner of his eye Tex saw him raising his knife. He grabbed the man's hand with his left, trying to force him to let go of the weapon. He was stronger than Tex, though.

"Who sent you?" he panted.

"Trespassers must pay," the man intoned.

The knife was edging toward his throat. Tex lifted his own weapon and plunged it into the other man's heart.

He staggered to his feet as the man died. He barely managed to pull his own knife out of the body and he wiped it on the dead man's trousers. Then he stood and surveyed the river and the banks, searching for another attacker.

There was none, but he saw a dark object up the bank that looked like a canoe. With no other immediate threat in sight he returned his attention to the dead man. He was a big man and he had light colored hair. He didn't appear to be a native and he wasn't dressed as a park ranger so his comment about trespassers made no sense. Besides, what park ranger came after someone with a knife?

Tex checked the dead man's pockets, looking for any clue to the man's identity. He came up with a package of gum. Then, in the man's shirt pocket, covered in blood, he found something chillingly familiar. It was a card with the yellow Helenium flower pressed into it.

He felt a cold chill dance up his spine. He hadn't seen his attacker's face in Honolulu but he was sure this was a different man. One man carrying a card with a yellow flower on it could have meant nothing. It could have even been a coincidence that the meaning of the flower was "tear". But a second man carrying a card with the same yellow flower attacking after he'd found the second Tear was a pattern. Both men had attacked at night hours after he'd discovered one of the Tears.

Did someone else know about the Tears or did he just have the terrible luck to have incurred the wrath of some sort of cult? He didn't like the picture that was starting to present itself.

He turned and trudged up to the man's canoe and looked inside. All he found were canteens. He wondered if this man had been the one to kill his guide.

Frustrated at the lack of leads he returned to his own canoe. He drug the man's body back to the base of the cliff and then sat up in his own canoe, waiting for the dawn.

At first light Tex shoved the canoe back into the river and climbed in. It would be a few more hours before he reached his destination, and he wanted to be on his way as quickly as possible. He had no idea if the dead man had friends, but he didn't want to stick around to find out.

The changing light of sunrise played over the walls of the canyon, bathing them in brilliant hues. He barely noticed, though. It was an occupational hazard. He got to see some of the most fantastic sights in the world but was often too busy trying to stay alive to appreciate them.

He cast frequent glances behind him, but just as the day before, he couldn't see anyone following him. That clearly hadn't meant anything, though, since he had been attacked in the night even though he had seen noone following him before that.

As mid morning arrived he found himself scanning the cliffs even more anxiously for signs of a way out or of the hotel which he should be seeing. Finally, far ahead, he saw black dots moving down the side of one of the cliffs.

People, it had to be, which meant there was a trail and a way out.

He paddled with renewed vigor and a short while later pulled his canoe up onto the shore and watched as a mule train finished making its way down. It took a couple of hours and Tex chafed at the delay, eager to be out of the canyon. There was an older man with a scraggly beard who appeared to be the guide for a small group of tourists. He dismounted from his animal and stepped forward to greet Tex.

"Afternoon," the old man said.

"Afternoon," Tex replied. "You're a sight for sore eyes. Am I anywhere near the El Tovar hotel?"

The man nodded and pointed up the cliff. "It's right up there. That's where we came from this morning. We'll be heading back up in a couple of hours."

"Any chance you can take an extra with you?"

The old man scratched his chin. "I reckon you can ride Bessy. I always bring a spare mule on these trips just in case. I can't let you go up by yourself since you don't know the terrain, but if you can wait a couple of hours you can join us."

"I can wait," Tex assured him.

"Sorry, I don't have an extra lunch with me."

"That's okay," Tex said even though his stomach rumbled in protest.

"You sure you don't mind leaving your canoe?"

Tex shook his head. "Maybe someone else can use it at some point."

There was a hitching post at the base of the cliff and after tying up his own mule the old man helped his guests down one by one. There were seven in total. Two couples and a family of three. The little girl had her socks and shoes off and feet in the water before he could even blink.

One of the couples set off hiking down the river a bit, hauling an expensive looking camera with them. For his part Tex planned to stick to the guide like glue until they were out of the canyon.

As the tourists ate and explored Tex waited and it was two of the longest hours of his life. He was exhausted and the temptation to take a nap was great, but he didn't want to risk being left behind. When the time finally came to leave he was the first on his mule. Bessy flicked her ears a lot, clearly irritated that her journey back up was not going to be as easy as her journey down had been.

When they finally made it up to the rim Tex breathed a sigh of relief. A while later he and the others had surrendered their mules and were heading into the hotel.

He checked in at the front desk and got himself a room. He was hungry so he made a quick trip to the restroom and then settled into the dining room to get some dinner. Several other patrons kept glancing at him, clearly curious about his disheveled appearance, but they left him alone. He ate enough for two men and had six glasses of water before he was done.

Finished he went upstairs to get settled into his room. It was clean, had plenty of space and featured a view of the canyon. He had had his fill of the natural wonder, though, and quickly closed the curtains.

After getting washed up Tex desperately wanted to sleep. He took some pain medication. Both arms were throbbing in equal protest to the treatment they'd been put through in the last two days. Once the medication kicked in and started to take the edge off he settled down on the bed and pulled out his journal. Even though his hand and arm cramped frequently as he wrote he wanted to get it all down while it was still fresh in his mind.

He began to chronicle what had occurred in the last two days. When describing the inside of the cave, particularly the great room, he took his time, describing everything in as much detail as he could remember. He drew some rough sketches of the room indicating the placement of the different objects and relative distances to each other. He also did a rough sketch of the Buddha like idol.

When it came time to describe the wall which he had to put the Tear into to activate he flipped forward in his notes to see the hieroglyphics he had copied down. It was half-translated at best. It was likely that the writing was a tribute to the pharaoh buried inside the tomb or possibly even instructions on how to open it. Just in case, though, he should finish the job. After all that was the wall that the writing had appeared on when the stone was warm.

He still wasn't sure how the Tear had caused that to happen in the first place. He could have sworn he had tried putting it against a stone when he was at home without any results. Maybe it was a particular kind of rock in the cave or perhaps there was more to the Tear than he understood. At this point he was almost positive that was the case.

He had packed a hieroglyphs reference notebook he had put together back when he was in school in his satchel, anticipating that he might need to translate some Egyptian writing. He got it out and flipped it open. He was out of practice and it was slow going. When he had finally finished he read the writing that had appeared on the cave wall and felt a chill like a cold wind rush through him.

Three Tears are needed to reveal the truth. In death he protects the second as he did in life. Souls must pass through the door to take his charge. Only a conqueror can possess the third entombed in the land of his birth. The tears of man come at a cost but without the tears of a god all is lost.

Chapter 11

Tex reread the lines several times. It was true that the Tears of Man were coming at a cost. Twice now he'd gotten his hands on one and barely escaped with his life. It was a sad commentary on the occupational hazards of his job that he had long ago become less interested in figuring out who was trying to kill him and much more interested in figuring out how to stay one step ahead of them. Although he did find himself increasingly interested in figuring out why those men who wanted him dead were carrying the Helenium flower with them.

At the moment, though, what both worried and intrigued him was the reference the hieroglyphs made to the tears of a god. Was it possible that finding the three Tears of Man was only part of the challenge? He really hoped not. Much more of this might kill him. All he could do at this point was hope that Dr. Reid would have some insight about what tears of a god could be a reference to. He tried to put aside his concern over that for a moment, and instead turned his attention to the first part which referenced the third Tear he was seeking.

"Only a conqueror can possess the third entombed in the land of his birth," he read out loud.

Dr. Reid hadn't shared with him yet where the third Tear might be. He wondered why only a conqueror could possess the Tear. It didn't make much sense. Where would the land of his birth be? It couldn't reference the conqueror without the writing being prophetic and eliminating the possibility of any but a single, specific person being the conqueror. No, he had to think that "land of his birth" was a reference to the mummy that had been buried in that chamber. Unless Tex missed his guess the land of that man's birth would have been Egypt. If he had been born here then it rendered the saying somewhat absurd. Even if it was Egypt, though, that was an incredibly vague clue to its location. There were so many tombs, how would one know the right one?

He placed both the Tears on the table next to the bed and studied them for a moment. They looked identical. If there were any differences between the two of them they couldn't be seen by the naked eye.

After looking at them closely he tried pushing them together to see if anything happened while they were touching each other. He watched for ten minutes but the Tears remained dormant.

Exhaustion weighing him down he finally gave up for the night. Hopefully Dr. Reid would be able to help him shed more light on the subject. He put the Tears away. Then he angled the back of the chair in his room underneath the doorknob so that any unwanted intruders wouldn't be able to get in. Twice now he'd had his sleep interrupted by would be assassins wielding knives. Tonight he needed to get a lot more sleep than he had been.

He was surprised when he woke up several hours later that the morning had come and nothing had happened to interrupt his slumber. He had to admit it was a welcome change. He had washed out his clothes in the sink the night before and he was pleased to discover that they had dried enough to wear. He was already thinking of abandoning the clothes left behind at the hotel he had been staying at before starting the river trek. He didn't want to run into anyone who would ask him if he had ever found a guide or might make inquiries about Hank. Plus sooner or later someone, probably a ranger, would discover the two bodies along the river.

It wasn't worth the risk. Besides, now he had two Tears in his possession and every moment he delayed was another moment where something could go horribly wrong. After breakfast he would see about chartering a plane and get out of here while he could.

He went downstairs and headed to the dining room. No sooner had he stepped inside than he spotted a familiar figure sitting alone at one of the tables. Her flame red hair was unmistakable. He could only see part of her face in profile but it was enough to confirm his suspicions that it was Lena.

He swore and took a step backward, inadvertently bumping into a fair-haired man in expensive clothes who looked down his nose at Tex. "Using such language in the presence of ladies is inexcusable," he said gruffly.

There were no ladies within earshot who could have heard him and he bit back his retort with an effort. The last thing he needed was a scene, and calling the other guy a lady would certainly lead to one. Instead he just grimaced and stepped behind a potted tree that was nearby. The other man rolled his eyes in disgust and continued into the dining room.

Tex should be going, but something kept him lingering there for a moment, watching. To his surprise the blond man headed straight to Lena's table. He kissed her hand

and then sat down opposite her. Curiosity roared through him. The man was too young to be her boss. Who was he then? A potential buyer or seller of antiquities? His wardrobe certainly indicated that he had wealth. Perhaps a friend or lover?

A waiter paused and looked at Tex. "May I get you anything, sir?"

"No, I've lost my appetite," Tex said, turning to go.

It struck him that this would be a good opportunity to try and find out more about the mysterious redhead and her even more elusive boss. He passed by a small sitting area that had a bouquet of flowers arranged in a vase on a side table. He glanced around to make sure no one was watching then pulled the flowers out of the vase, shaking the ends slightly to get rid of the excess water. Then he headed straight for the front desk. Fortunately the clerk there was not the same one that had checked him in yesterday.

"May I help you?" the clerk said with a friendly smile.

Tex grinned as hard as he could. "I hope so. I'm here to surprise my wife on vacation. I'm supposed to be working, but I managed to close the deal I was working on and here I am. Her name is Lena Jenkins."

He was hoping that she was going by the same name she had given him on the train.

The clerk quickly consulted his book. "Yes, Mrs. Jenkins checked in just an hour ago. Room 312."

"312. I can't wait to see the look on her face," Tex said.

He turned and headed off to the elevator. He first stopped at his room and was relieved to find it untouched. He grabbed his satchel which contained everything that was currently important to him including both his gun and hers from the train and a lock pick set. When he found her room it was simple for him to pick the lock. Once inside he set the flowers and the satchel down and began to look around.

The more cautious side of his nature was screaming at him to take this opportunity to get out of the hotel before Lena found him. He had too much to lose by risking another confrontation with her. His curiosity was too great, though. He had to find out if there was anything else he could discover about her or her boss. If there was one thing he'd learned the hard way in his years in the field it was that knowledge was power. Given that her boss seemed to know an awful lot about Tex, at the moment the scales were most definitely tipped in their favor. He was looking for anything he could find that would help balance things out.

She had a new suitcase filled with clothes. He couldn't detect any hidden compartments in it. He put it back in the closet and continued to look around, but didn't see anything. He had half expected to find a card with the yellow flower in her possession as well, but he didn't.

She was probably keeping anything important or valuable on her. He hadn't been able to see if she had a purse with her in the dining room, but given that there wasn't any kind of wallet in the room he figured she had to have something like that with her.

He didn't find a gun in the room either. That meant she hadn't had time to replace the one he'd taken from her on the train or she was also carrying it with her.

Frustrated that it had been a waste of time he picked up the flowers and the satchel and headed for the door. Once there he paused as he heard voices outside in the hall. He'd wait until it was clear before heading out. The voices grew more distinct and with a sinking feeling he recognized one of them as belonging to Lena.

There was no way to exit the room without being caught. So the trick would be getting caught in the best possible way for him. He quickly pulled his gun out of the satchel and tucked it in the back of his waistband. Then he slid his satchel under the bed, just out of sight. Still holding the flowers he lounged back on the bed, adopting an air of waiting.

A moment later the door opened. Lena had her head turned as she walked in, talking to the blond man who was right behind her. "As I said, I'm sure we can work out an arrange-"

She turned and jumped slightly, eyes wide. Most women would have screamed at finding a man in their room so unexpectedly. He had to admire her for the control she had.

"Hello, lover," he said, slowly sitting up. "Did you miss me?" he asked.

"What are you doing here?"

He smiled. "Isn't it obvious?"

"What is the meaning of this?" the blond man sputtered, his face turning red.

Her hand was sliding inside a clutch purse she was holding. He figured the only thing that had kept her from pulling a weapon out was the presence of the other man. He could use that to his advantage.

"That's what I should be asking," Tex said, glaring at him.

He stood and walked over to them. Her hand was still inside her purse. “I brought these for you,” he said, thrusting the flowers toward her.

She was forced to remove her hand from her purse to take them and while she did he snatched the purse from her. In one move he removed the tiny derringer she’d had in there, pocketed it, and threw her purse on the bed.

He made a show of looking the other man over from head to toe. “I wouldn’t have thought he was your type.

“You, sir, are no gentleman,” the other guy fumed.

“Never claimed to be,” Tex said. He retrieved his satchel from under the bed and slung it over his shoulder. He headed for the door and they both moved out of his way. He turned and locked eyes with the man. “Seeing as how you are, though, I’ll just give you a friendly warning. Watch this one. She likes to play rough.”

The man began to sputter and Lena just shook her head. Tex couldn’t tell if she was angry or amused, but he suspected it was a bit of both. Either way it was time to leave while he still could.

He stepped into the hall, closed the door, and ran for the stairs. He had no idea if either one of them would be giving chase, but he wasn’t sticking around to find out. Fortunately for him a taxi was waiting outside the front entrance to the hotel. He slid in the back. “I need to get to the nearest airfield,” he said.

The driver looked at him and hesitated.

“What’s wrong?” Tex asked.

“I’m supposed to be picking up someone else, but they’re already late.”

“I’ll give you double your fare.”

"And they're out of luck," the driver said, turning around and starting the car up.

Tex glanced back at the hotel as they left it behind. Lena had looked genuinely surprised to see him. Maybe she hadn't realized that they were at the same hotel. It was also possible she had been serious about Arizona being her destination when she'd told him that on the train. He was willing to bet, though, that whoever the man was he was most certainly not her cousin.

He couldn't help but wonder what had been going on with Lena and the blond man. Whatever it was he hoped that he had spoiled her plans.

She, on the other hand, had cost him something by coming back to her room before he could vacate it. He'd had to leave behind his new hat. He sighed. When he got back home he'd have to buy another one.

When he made it to the airfield it took a little bit of haggling, but he finally found a pilot willing to fly him all the way back home. The entire time the plane was being fueled and the pilot was running through his safety checks, Tex found himself watching the road to the airfield, waiting to see if Lena or another man with a yellow flower was coming after him.

No one had by the time the pilot was ready to go. Still it was with relief that Tex buckled himself into his seat, his satchel in his hands. With two Tears now in his possession and far more questions than he'd had before he arrived here he couldn't wait to get back home.

All told it took a couple of stops and nearly a day to get back to Washington D.C. and Tex was bone-numbingly tired by the time they landed at the airfield. He got a taxi and had it take him straight home. He'd wash up, get some sleep, and then hopefully see Dr. Reid late that afternoon at the library. Although he was beginning to think that a discussion somewhere more private might be in order.

When the car pulled up in front of his house he dragged himself out of it and made his way to the front door. He walked in, flicked on a light, and came to an abrupt halt in his trek toward the bedroom.

Everywhere he looked things were in disarray. Papers were dumped all over the floor, furniture had been tipped over, and not a drawer remained untouched. Everything he owned appeared to be dumped into huge piles, one in the center of each room.

He groaned in anger and frustration. He didn't know why he was surprised. His place had been thoroughly searched and torn apart.

"Not again," he groaned as he stared around at the mess.

Then he heard something fall over upstairs. He grabbed his gun and tossed his satchel onto the overturned kitchen table as he walked past. He held the gun in both hands as he crept toward the stairs. Someone was still in the house.

He made it up the narrow steps, stepping over the sixth one which always creaked so it wouldn't give him away. He made it onto the upstairs landing and turned toward his closed study door. He was pretty sure the sound had come from in there.

He waited a moment, back pressed to the wall, listening. He could hear light shuffling inside. He positioned himself carefully in front of the door, gun at the ready.

With one swift kick the door went flying inward. Before Tex could step inside something leaped out at him, hitting him hard in the chest.

Chapter 12

Tex backpedalled and slammed into the wall. The creature that had assaulted him dropped onto the ground. He stared down at the fluffy gray cat in shock.

"Who are you and where did you come from?" he asked.

The cat looked up at him and meowed in obvious distress. Tex stepped around him and checked his study. It had been ransacked like the rest of the house, and he stared in anger at some of the older, more fragile books that had been dumped unceremoniously on the floor. Whoever had done this had no respect.

He felt a tapping on his leg and he looked down to see the cat staring up at him with huge yellow eyes. Tex wondered how long the poor fellow had been trapped in there. He turned and popped his head into the bedroom which was also a disaster before heading downstairs.

The cat raced down ahead of him and was waiting at the front door when he got there. He opened it and let the fluffy creature out. It raced straight to the flower beds. Tex shook his head as he closed the door. The cat must have wondered in when his home was being trashed and accidentally been locked in upstairs. Of course, it was possible that whoever had done this thought that the cat belonged to him. Well, at least it was free now to return to whatever worried owner was missing him.

Tex moved into the kitchen and moved his satchel before righting the table. He then set the satchel back down on top of it. His mind was whirring as he thought of all of the work ahead of him. He'd have to go through and make sure the thieves hadn't taken anything. Although he was pretty sure that what they were looking for had been with him all along. He didn't even bother calling the police. This wasn't some local criminal who they'd be able to catch trying to sell his stuff.

The question was, who had searched his place? An associate of Lena's? One of the men with the Helenium flower? He was getting tired of not knowing who all the players were and what their motivations could be.

He heard a sudden scratching at his front door. Maybe the cat had gotten confused and gone to the wrong house. He moved through the kitchen, straightening a few things as he went. The scratching continued getting louder and more persistent.

Finally Tex went to the front door and opened it. The gray cat pushed past him and headed for the kitchen. Tex closed the door and followed him. "Excuse me, this isn't your house," he told the cat.

The cat jumped onto the table, sat down, and stared at him.

"What is it you want?" Tex asked.

The cat continued to stare intently.

He wants food, Tex realized.

The cat wasn't his responsibility, but he felt bad that it had been locked in his house for heaven only knew how long. With a sigh he went into the kitchen and found a can of tuna in one of the cupboards. He opened it and returned to the table where he set the can down in front of the cat.

The cat glanced at it then back at him. Tex stared back. “It’s tuna. I thought cats liked fish? Besides, you should be starving and happy to have anything.”

And now he was talking to a cat.

His stomach rumbled as he looked at the tuna. It had been more than a day since he’d eaten anything. He went back to the cupboard, and grabbed a can for himself. He opened it, grabbed a fork and sat down at the table.

“Cheers,” he said, lifting the can in the air slightly.

He dug his fork in to his can and as soon as he lifted the first bite to his lips the cat dipped his head and began to eat out of his can.

“You are one weird cat,” he said around the food in his mouth.

After finishing his tuna Tex got up to get himself some water. He brought a small bowl of water over for the cat, too.

Tex realized he was beginning to nod off. He needed to get at least a few hours sleep before he did anything else. The thieves had torn apart his bed upstairs and it was going to take a lot of effort to put it all back together again. Instead he stood up and went into the living room where he was able to flip the couch back over with relative ease. He kicked off his shoes and stretched out on it.

A moment later the cat jumped up and laid down on his chest, staring intently at him. Tex eyed him, too tired to do anything about it. “You are not my cat,” he said.

The animal kept staring at him, as though refusing to be the first one to blink.

“As long as you understand that,” Tex said, his words already sounding slurred.

Several hours later he woke to a low rumbling sound. He was aware of a weight on his chest and left shoulder as he slowly opened his eyes. The gray cat was there, stretched out, his head close to Tex's chin, purring deeply.

"Dang it. I'm going to have to give you a name," Tex said softly.

The cat made a little trilling noise but kept sleeping.

He glanced over at the clock on the wall. It was almost four in the afternoon. "Unfortunately, that's going to have to wait. I have a man to see first."

He eased the sleeping cat up and the animal mewed but allowed himself to be placed down on the couch where he resumed sleeping. Apparently he was even more tired than Tex had been.

He went upstairs, washed up and got some clean clothes on. In his button down white shirt and gray slacks he was looking more like the academic than the adventurer. Given that he was headed to the library that was a good thing.

Half an hour later he was walking to the back of the library. The place was more empty than normal and he could hear his footsteps echoing, the sound bouncing off the walls. By the time he reached the back table that Dr. Reid frequented he would have been surprised if the whole building hadn't been alerted to his presence.

When he rounded the last bookcase that obscured his view he saw Dr. Reid, half-risen from his chair, looking his way with a look of agitation on his face. When he saw Tex a look of relief broke out on his face and he stood completely, a smile on his features.

When Tex reached him Dr. Reid clapped him on the back enthusiastically before sitting back down. “You don’t know how relieved I am to see you,” he said.

The cat who had been on the table jumped onto Dr. Reid’s lap and Tex couldn’t help but briefly wonder if the two of them had even left the library since he’d seen them last.

He sat down across the table from them and made himself comfortable.

“So, you found it, did you?” Dr. Reid asked with a gleam in his eyes.

“I did,” Tex admitted.

“I knew it!” Dr. Reid chortled and pounded his fist on the table.

The move startled Tex who rarely had seen his mentor this excited about something.

“Do you want to see it?” Tex asked cautiously.

The other man quickly shook his head. “No, keep it put away. I trust it looks like the other one?”

“It’s twin.”

“As it should. Very good.”

“You should have seen the place, Professor,” Tex said. “I never would have believed it if I hadn’t seen it with my own eyes.”

“I take it that it was as the article described?”

“And more. You were right about looking for a royal burial, by the way. I found a hidden chamber. The pharaoh was buried with some of the most amazing things I’ve ever seen. What was most amazing was it took the first Tear to even access the chamber and both Tears to get back out.”

Dr. Reid nodded, seeming to hang on his every word.

Tex leaned back. "But the enormity of everything I found. I'd love to take a team and spend a couple of months exploring and cataloguing the place. Who knows, maybe next summer I could get the university to sponsor a dig and the archaeology students can get their field school experience there. It would be an amazing project."

"It would at that," Dr. Reid said, sounding somewhat wistful.

Tex cocked his head to the side. "You don't think it will happen, do you?"

"Sadly no. The Smithsonian expedition was swept under the carpet and I don't see you being able to persuade a government official to give you access to the site...officially."

Tex shook his head. "What I saw there could rewrite what we think we know about our history."

"And there are a lot of people who are frightened by that thought, some of them quite powerful. Remember, knowledge-"

"Is power," Tex said with a sigh. "I know."

"I'm sorry. It hurts me, too. Before we begin to bemoan the deplorable state of truth, history, and science as they relate to each other, tell me more about your trip."

"It ended up being far more eventful than I was hoping for."

"Oh?"

"Yeah. For starters I was accosted on the train by a very interesting lady who tried to sweet talk me into going on a quest for her boss to find the Spear of Destiny. Turns out her real mission was to steal the Tear, although she didn't know what it was. She thought she was looking for a gemstone."

Dr. Reid's eyes had opened wide. "Did this lady have a name?"

"Lena Jenkins. I have no idea if that's her real name or not."

"Lena Jenkins."

"You ever hear the name?" Tex asked.

"I'm afraid I don't know the lady in question," the professor said.

"I managed to part ways with her, but she showed up again, this time in Arizona the morning I was leaving."

"Interesting."

"Disturbing is more like it. What I didn't like was how much her boss seemed to know about me."

"In some circles you are becoming quite well known."

"Not like this. This was much more...personal," Tex said grimly.

"You said 'for starters'. I take it she was not the only obstacle you encountered?"

"No, a man tried to kill me."

"Oh my!"

"And he was carrying the same Helenium flower card as the man in Hawaii who tried to kill me."

"But I take it they were not the same man?"

"No, two different guys. And the first one is still alive out there somewhere," Tex said grimly.

Dr. Reid shook his head. "I tried to do some digging, but I didn't find anything about a group that uses the Helenium flower as their symbol."

"So, we're either dealing with a very small group or a very secretive one."

"It could also be a relatively new group."

Tex shook his head. "I don't think so. That's not what my gut is telling me. I think these guys have been around a while and we just haven't heard about them."

"So, something like a secret society perhaps?"

"That's what I'm thinking."

"I'll take another crack at it from that angle, see if there isn't anything I can find out."

"I appreciate that, Professor," Tex said.

The cat jumped on the table for a drink of water and Tex watched him for a moment.

"It seems I've been adopted by a cat as well," he said absently.

Dr. Reid smiled. "They can be excellent companions if you're well-suited to each other."

"I guess we'll find out. While I was gone someone ransacked my house and somehow this cat got in there and was locked in my office. Now he won't leave."

"Was anything taken?" Dr. Reid asked, concern heavy in his voice.

"I don't know yet, but they made a heck of a mess. I'm guessing they were after the same thing Lena was. I just wish I knew how someone other than the two of us is aware that I have the Tears," he said, locking eyes with the other man.

It had been bothering him ever since the train. How had Lena's boss known what he was carrying. Noone but Dr. Reid should know. The man was about ten years older than he was, not old in his eyes, but the thought occurred to him that Lena might think of Dr. Reid as old, particularly since he used a walking stick because of his limp.

He didn't like the suspicions that were filling him about his mentor, but the man was the only other soul who knew.

"I haven't told anyone," Dr. Reid said.

"Not even the person you said you could get the tablet from that talks about the Tears."

"No, not even him. I was waiting to talk to him to see if you brought back the second Tear or if we were just on a wild goose chase. I haven't talked to a soul."

"And neither have I," Tex said, staring hard at the other man.

It took a moment, but Dr. Reid finally seemed to understand that Tex was all but accusing him of having sent Lena to steal the Tear from him. Anger flashed in the other man's eyes just for a moment followed by what Tex could only think was sorrow.

"You think I've betrayed you," Dr. Reid said, his voice heavy sounding.

"You wouldn't be the first," he answered, struggling to keep the bitterness out of his voice.

"But why? I'm the one who told you what I suspected it was and pointed you in the direction of the second."

"Yeah, and you always know more about anything than you'll say."

"If I wanted the Tear for some reason, I would have asked you for it," Dr. Reid said.

Tex blinked and dropped his eyes. "And I probably would have given it to you," he admitted. It was true. He'd always had so much respect for the other man. That coupled with a deep desire not to get pulled into something as outlandish as this would have made it easy to hand over the Tear in the beginning and wash his hands of the whole matter.

"I have no need to steal from you," Dr. Reid said earnestly. "It pains me that you think I do."

"I'm sorry," Tex said, taking a deep breath. "But you can see how nothing else really makes sense?"

"I see why you jumped to the conclusion you did. It doesn't mean I have to like it."

"Okay, who else could possibly know? I mean, I've been trying to figure this out for days and I just keep coming up blank. No one should know."

"It's possible that someone knew that a Tear was hidden on Kauai and has been watching you since you visited that spot," the other man suggested.

That would, at least, make some sense. And it was in Hawaii before he'd had a chance to even talk to Dr. Reid that the first man had attacked him.

"You're right, of course, that has to be it," he said contritely.

"It's okay, Charles," Dr. Reid said with a smile. "We all make mistakes from time-to-time and even the best of us occasionally have a hard time distinguishing between friend and foe. Now, we'll work on figuring out who these Helenium flower people might be later. Now let's discuss the third Tear?"

"Do you know where it is?"

"No, but I'm betting that working together, we can figure it out," Dr. Reid said with a small smile.

"That sounds good. I found a clue to its location when I found the second one. There were hieroglyphs on the wall to the secret chamber, and they talked about the Tears."

"What did they say?" Dr. Reid asked, leaning forward intently.

"It said-"

The cat hissed and laid its ears flat back on its head and arched its back. Before he or the professor could move or say anything else Tex heard a shout coming from the front of the library. A moment later he heard a single word loud and clear.

"Fire!"

Chapter 13

Tex jumped to his feet and ran toward the front of the library. When he was almost there he could smell smoke and a moment later he could see it rising from the left side near the entrance.

People were running out the front door as he raced up. On the wall inside the door was mounted a fire extinguisher which he grabbed. He turned and ran toward the source of the smoke and moments later saw flames.

When he got close he realized that the flames were shooting up out of a metal wastepaper basket. He took aim with the fire extinguisher and doused the flames. When he had emptied the extinguisher he dropped it and turned toward the entrance where people were still pushing against one another trying to get out.

"It's okay! The fire's out!" he called, but no one seemed to be listening.

Suddenly in the midst of the crowd he caught a flash of bright, red hair. He started forward. It couldn't be. Then he lost sight of the red splash as more people pressed outside.

He rushed forward and pushed his way into the crowd, fighting to get out through the doors. Once he had finally made it through he scanned the crowd frantically. People were scurrying away from the building in all directions.

There, he saw a flash of red hair again in a small knot of people that were disappearing around the right side of the building. He leaped forward then collided with a couple of hysterical young girls who were fleeing the library. He lost valuable seconds making sure they were okay before he was able to run around the side of the building.

There were a couple of smaller classroom buildings facing the side of the library and there were at least twenty people scattered between him and them. None of them had red hair, though.

Then he saw the edge of a woman's skirt as its owner disappeared inside the nearest building. He sprinted forward, determined not to let her get away. He ran into the building and looked left then right but didn't see anyone. Then he heard footsteps on the staircase that started straight in front of him and quickly angled to the left.

He ran up the stairs two at a time and at the top saw movement in the doorway at the far end of the hall. He sprinted down the hall, ran into the room, and grabbed the arm of a woman who was walking into a closet.

She screamed as he yanked her out of the closet. It wasn't Lena. In fact this girl didn't even have red hair.

"Sorry," he said, dropping her arm. "Thought you were someone else."

He turned and hurried out of the room. He made it downstairs and back outside where he again looked around. There were no redheads anywhere in sight. He had lost her, he realized with mounting frustration. He turned slowly and headed back toward the library.

People were still gathered outside and a fire truck was just pulling up. Tex managed to get in the door before one of the firemen could start blocking access. He made his way back over to the wastepaper basket which still had a thick layer of smoke around it.

Moments later he was joined by a couple of the firemen. "This was where the fire was?" the one asked him.

"Yeah, it was in the basket. I put it out with the extinguisher there," Tex said, indicating the empty canister.

"Quick thinking."

The second man bent down and with a gloved hand inspected the remnants of the burnt papers. After a minute he looked up. "Looks like someone threw in a cigarette butt. It wasn't properly put out and the papers caught. Just an accident."

Tex would stake everything he had that it hadn't been an accident. He kept silent, though. No need to draw these men into what they would undoubtedly think was either a prank or a crazy conspiracy theory.

"I'm just glad I could help," he said before walking away.

Had it really been Lena he had seen? If so, what had been her plan? Had she been trying to draw him out? If so, then why would she have run and not lured him into some sort of a trap?

He was sure that the fire had been set deliberately, but he didn't understand what the objective could have been. He was fine, and no one had come after him or the Tears that he had in his pocket. It would seem like a failed attempt to lure him out.

He blinked. Unless it was all about luring him away so that she could get at Dr. Reid.

He turned and sprinted toward the back of the library, hoping that nothing had happened to Dr. Reid. When he passed the last stack that blocked his view his heart skipped a beat and he staggered to a halt.

Dr. Reid and his cat were gone.

Tex walked forward slowly. When he had run for the front of the library Dr. Reid hadn't so much as gotten up, at least, not that he'd seen. And he wasn't among the people out front just now. Had he been kidnapped?

The man's papers, briefcase, and walking stick were missing as well. Only the library books remained, stacked in neat little piles all over the desk. He was clenching his fists as he tried to think through what Lena could possibly want with Dr. Reid when his eyes spied a piece of paper on the chair that the Dr. had been sitting on.

He picked up the piece of paper. There were words scrawled on it in Dr. Reid's handwriting, and he felt himself breathe a sigh of relief. The paper read: *Tomorrow 2 p.m. here.*

He slipped the note in his pocket. Dr. Reid and his cat were alright after all. "Well, look at that. They *can* leave the library," Tex mused.

A minute later he tensed up. He hated waiting and that's all he was doing now. Waiting for his next meeting with Dr. Reid. Waiting for Lena to strike again. Waiting to see if another man with a knife and a yellow flower came for him. It was like he was in the middle of some horrible triangle, waiting for someone, anyone, to make a move.

Patience had never been his strong suit and already he could feel his frustration mounting. There had to be something proactive he could do in the meantime. After a minute of thinking he sighed and shook his head. Probably the best thing he could do was go home and reread Plato.

He briefly thought about trying to track down Dr. Reid at home, but the man had set an appointment for tomorrow and probably with good reason. No matter how much he hated it, he would just have to wait.

He looked at all the books stacked on the desk. He thought about the librarian who seemed to intensely dislike the cat. He wondered if she scurried around putting away the books every day after Dr. Reid left or if she left his table alone.

He idly picked up a couple of the books, perusing titles. It looked like Dr. Reid was doing research on mythology and ancient Egyptian history. He wondered if the research was connected to the Tears or some other pet project the man was studying.

He picked up one of the books and glanced at the title. *Mythology and the Psyche.* He did a double take as he read the author's name. *Dr. Nicholas Reid.* Why was the doctor reading a book he himself had authored? Maybe he'd take a look and see if he could figure out what the other man was looking for.

He tucked the book under his arm and headed for the front of the library. There was still some commotion, but the firefighters were letting those who wanted to return to the library in the front door. Without looking to the right or the left Tex made straight for it and walked out unchallenged with the book in his possession.

Once outside he turned his steps toward home. He suddenly had a lot more reading to do, and he was eager to get started. As he walked he kept looking for signs of an elusive redhead, but saw nothing that would arouse suspicion. That in itself was almost enough to make him suspicious.

Before he reached home he realized that there were some things he needed to pick up and he headed instead to the grocery store. Inside a nice young woman was very much of assistance in helping him pick up everything he would need for the new cat in his life. He also made sure to pick up several cans of tuna for both of them as well as a few things for himself.

At last, juggling several heavy bags, he left the grocery store and made it the rest of the way home. Inside he dropped the bags on the kitchen table and looked around at the disaster that still remained. He had forgotten that he had hours if not days of work ahead of him just trying to put the place back together.

He began putting away the groceries and set up the litter box for the cat. Once he had finished he opened some more tuna for both of them and the cat once again joined him at the table.

As they ate Tex looked the cat over more carefully. He really was a beautiful animal with medium-long fur that fluffed out around him. He was all grey except for two patches of white. Both back paws and partway up the legs were white, giving the impression that he was wearing white boots on his hind legs.

"Fuzzyboots. That's your name," Tex said.

The cat looked up from his tuna and meowed as though in response.

"See, you already know your name," Tex said with a smile.

After he finished eating he headed upstairs to at least repair some of the damage done to his office. He re-shelved the books with care as protecting the more fragile tomes was the important task before him. When he was finished with that he went and put his bed back together, stacking the mattress on top of the box springs. He was just grateful that whoever had searched the place hadn't slashed them open looking for something he might have sown inside.

With some semblance of order returning to the upstairs he took a shower and then settled on the bed with Dr. Reid's mythology book. He hadn't been sitting more than a minute when Fuzzyboots jumped up to join him and curled up next to his leg.

He gave the cat's head a scratch. "Okay, so apparently I have a cat," he said, admitting it. He wasn't sure how that had happened, but he liked the furry fellow and was glad that the cat had come to him, regardless of how it had happened.

He flipped quickly through the book, looking for any markings the professor might have made. The text was clean, though, and there didn't appear to be any bookmarks either.

He sighed and started at the beginning. He had to admit that his mentor did have a very engaging writing style and frequently made excellent points. He was writing, though, in generalities about how mankind, no matter how different people seemed the world over, shared a core group of fundamental stories. These fundamental stories were repeated the world over throughout history by people that would have had no contact with each other. He listed creation myths, flood myths, and end of the world myths as three myths or beliefs common to the human experience regardless of if you were talking about the ancient Greeks or the American Indian tribes. He proposed that there was a need in the human psyche to answer the questions "Where did we come from?" and "Where are we going?"

After that it started to get more interesting. The professor discussed flood myths and postulated that the fact that the same myth was shared by all ancient cultures might actually be seen as evidence that such a cataclysm had indeed occurred at one point in time. He then went on to state that other types of myths and stories that shared similar universal connections should be examined more closely for the truth.

That was when Dr. Reid mentioned Atlantis.

Tex found himself sitting up straighter as he began to devour what the professor had to say about the myth of a lost civilization. He pointed to similar stories shared by several cultures besides the Greeks. Some of them even had names that were somewhat similar to Atlantis.

There were a couple of different cities or lands in the mythology of India with some of the descriptions both of the place and its denizens being similar. Dr. Reid went on to discuss Aztlan, the place where the Aztecs believe they settled on after emerging from the earth. Aztlan was destroyed and sunk beneath the sea. The Toltecs also believed that they came from a lost island called Aztlan.

Tex was surprised to discover that Plato wasn't the first to write about Atlantis. The Greek writer Hellanicus had a writing entitled "Atlantis" which was written well before Plato's account. Unfortunately the text did not survive intact but had been referenced by other writers.

Dr. Reid had laid out an amazing amount of evidence, even if it was circumstantial. Clearly he'd had more than just a passing interest in the lost continent for a long time. Tex kept reading but there seemed to be no reference in the book to the Tears of Man or even to orichalcum itself.

Dr. Reid went on to speculate that even though lost island or continent myths were prevalent in the ancient world that the modern one would likely not embrace the concept unless presented with proof of the existence of Atlantis, either by way of discovering the place itself or discovering ancient references to it on Egyptian monuments.

When Plato told the story of Atlantis, he claimed that Solon was the one who heard it from priests of Neith in Sais, Egypt while traveling there. The record of Atlantis was shown to Solon and was carved as hieroglyphs into a column. That made sense since it was known that Solon had traveled there in his lifetime, and it was not uncommon for Greeks to do so. According to Plato the Egyptian priests told Solon that the Greeks had no concept of the antiquity of their own history. They claimed that instead of one great flood there had been several, each wiping out civilizations and the histories that went with them, leaving behind only the uneducated who had to create civilization all over again and who had no memory of what had gone before. They claimed that Egyptians had survived these floods and that their history contained records of other civilizations.

Dr. Reid speculated if a column such as that which detailed the history of Atlantis could be found in Egypt and verified as predating Plato, then it would become harder for the story of Atlantis to be dismissed as a political allegory fabricated by Plato and that researchers would have to investigate it in a serious manner instead of just dismissing it out of hand.

Tex reread that section several times. Dr. Reid was right, discovery of such a column would make it harder to discount the story of Atlantis as set forth by Plato. Of course, the real question was, did such a column exist? Even if it had at one time it could have since been destroyed by any number of things or been swallowed up by the sands forever. Finding it would be difficult, but it could help change the entire landscape of their history.

Tex closed the book after the section on Atlantis seemed to have come to an end. He wondered what more Dr. Reid might be able to tell him about the column and its location. Instead of gaining some answers reading the book had just left him with more questions.

Of course, it would all be a moot point if he managed to find the third Tear and the three Tears together did provide the location for Atlantis. He took a minute to just stop and think what that would even mean.

It would change everything: history, archaeology, metallurgy, even electricity if the Tears were any indication of what the ancient Atlanteans might have achieved. Given what he'd seen the Tears accomplish he couldn't help but wonder what other strange and unusual technologies the ancient culture that fashioned them might have created.

If he could find it he wouldn't have to imagine. He'd be able to see it for himself firsthand. The world would change and they might even be able to make some huge advancements in a short amount of time.

He felt himself growing excited thinking about the endless possibilities. He was always used to looking, thinking, half the time even living in the past. If he found Atlantis, though, he could be doing something that would tremendously impact the future, not only for him but for all mankind.

A sudden thought flashed into his mind. He thought about his discussion with Dr. Reid about the lost Egyptian city in the Grand Canyon and the fact that its existence had not yet come to light and might never if some parties had their way.

Knowledge was power.

Atlantean knowledge in the wrong hands could be the destruction of the world instead of its salvation. Either way it would be upsetting the balance. That would make some people very unhappy. Maybe even unhappy enough to kill to keep it from happening.

Maybe that had something to do with the men of the yellow flower. Maybe they were somehow working to suppress the knowledge of Atlantis and keep it hidden forever. If that was true, then he realized they'd never stop until he was dead.

Chapter 14

Tex's sleep was haunted by fitful dreams and shadowy figures all having red hair and carrying yellow flowers. When the morning came he woke somber and more worried about the Tears in his possession than he had been when he went to sleep.

He realized he needed a more secure way to carry them than wrapped in a handkerchief. He needed to conceal them in such a way that he could get to them but they could not be easily found by others. It had been nothing short of a miracle that Lena had overlooked the one in the handkerchief that day on the train. He'd not be likely to be so lucky if such a thing should happen again.

After breakfast he reread Plato's accounts of Atlantis as he'd originally planned to do the night before. Finished with that he continued to put his house back together. He had done a decent job and was able to grab a light lunch before heading back to the library to meet up with Dr. Reid. He grabbed the book he had taken from the library the night before on his way out.

On his way there he kept a sharp eye out for anyone suspicious but didn't see anything. The library still had the slightest hint of a smoke smell in the air when he walked inside. People were there, though, busily doing research and it was as if the excitement of the day before had never happened.

He couldn't forget, though, and as he made his way to the back of the building he could feel his chest tightening slightly in anxiety, hoping that Dr. Reid was there and that nothing had happened to him.

When the table finally came into sight he could feel himself relax. Sitting there, as though he had never moved, was Dr. Reid. This time, though, the cat was actually napping on the table, stretched out on his side. Tex was surprised his arrival hadn't caused the cat to awaken.

He slid into the seat across from Dr. Reid and put the book on the table.

"I was wondering who had dared to touch my books," Dr. Reid said, reaching out and retrieving it."

"You left in a hurry yesterday," Tex noted.

"Given the commotion I thought it an opportune time to go. What happened, by the way?"

"Someone threw a cigarette butt into a wastepaper basket at the front of the building."

"How incredibly careless."

"Actually, I'm pretty sure it was done on purpose. I used the fire extinguisher near the door to put it out and I caught a glimpse of what I think was Lena exiting with the rest of the crowd. I chased after, but I lost her."

"How did you know it was her?"

"I saw a bit of her hair. She has bright red hair, very distinctive."

"Ah," Dr. Reid said, looking a bit perplexed.

"Why, what's wrong?" Tex asked.

"Nothing. It just seems extraordinary that she would have been able to track you all the way here and so quickly, too."

"I know. I thought the same thing, but the woman is persistent, and she clearly has resources."

Dr. Reid tapped the book as he placed it back in one of his stacks. "Read anything interesting?" he asked drily.

"A lot. Perhaps the most interesting thing was realizing just how long you've bought into the Atlantis myth."

Dr. Reid gave him a thin smile. "An old adage that is particularly apropos given yesterday's events fits here. Where there is smoke, there is fire."

"I'm surprised you didn't mention anything about the legend of the Tears."

"Just because I believe that there was an Atlantis and would like others to doesn't mean I was prepared to share everything I knew with the masses."

"Or with some of the more aggressive grave robbers who might have come asking questions you couldn't or wouldn't answer?"

"Something like that. What's important is that two Tears have been found, and by the right person."

"I appreciate the vote of confidence," Tex said.

"Even as a student, you were remarkable. I always knew you'd do great things," Dr. Reid said, looking proud.

"Sometimes great things and crazy things look a lot alike."

"It is true. It ensures that only those who dare to appear crazy may achieve the truly great. Nature's way of rewarding the bold I guess."

"Tell me the truth. You've been waiting for one of these Tears to pop up, haven't you? I mean I know at the university you have a reputation for knowing everything about everything, but I think this has been more than just a passive bit of knowledge collecting on your part. You knew that Tear was in the Grand Canyon."

"I highly suspected."

"Then why didn't you go after it yourself long before this?"

"Who says I didn't try once upon a time?" Dr. Reid reached out and for a moment caressed the top of his walking stick which was propped up against the table.

"Your rafting accident," Tex realized suddenly.

Dr. Reid sighed. "Alas, it was no accident."

"You never made it inside the cave, did you?"

"No. When I woke up in the hospital it was a month later and I would never walk the same again, let alone manage to get up the cliff."

"You could have sent someone else in your place."

"Come, Charles, who would I have trusted with such a thing but you? The Tears are too important and the quest too dangerous for someone else."

"I'm not sure if I should be flattered or furious."

"Be flattered. It's better for both of us. Tell me, though, more about the caves that you found."

"Yes, the whole thing was amazing. And the room that I found the Tear in never could have been seen by the Smithsonian expedition. There was a full Egyptian burial. I only had a few hours so I couldn't see much, but I'm guessing those caves hold treasures we can't even imagine."

"We know that to be true. You managed to liberate one of those treasures."

Tex shook his head. "So, where do we go from here? I assume you have a theory about the location of the third Tear? If not this whole thing will have been for nothing."

"The third Tear. Yes, well, I've been giving that some thought."

"As have I." Tex reached into his pocket and pulled out the piece of paper with the translated inscription on it. He had never gotten a chance to share it yesterday before the fire broke out.

The professor read it over several times and then looked up at Tex with a puzzled expression. "Have you figured out what it means yet?"

"About the location of the third Tear or what the devil it means by the tears of a god? No. I can't even figure out why it will take a conqueror to acquire the third. Hopefully that's not literal."

Reid put the piece of paper down on the table and tapped it absently with his fingers. "Interesting."

"I think the land of his birth part relates to the mummy I found. So, I'm thinking Egypt."

"It's a good guess and an accurate one."

"What do you know?" Tex asked.

"Do you remember that I mentioned to you that there was a tablet that mentioned the Tears?"

"Yes. Have you managed to acquire it?"

Reid smiled. "Indeed I have. Although I must say doing so required even more persuasion than I anticipated."

Tex couldn't help but wonder what that would have looked like. He didn't say anything, though, just nodded to indicate that the other man should continue.

"I've only had the opportunity to study the tablet for a couple of hours, but the keeper did provide me with a rough translation. From what I've read I'd say the third Tear is in Giza. The use of the word 'entombed' here leads me to believe-"

"It's in one of the pyramids," Tex interrupted.

"Precisely."

"That's going to be a big problem. Even if I could find the right pyramid and the right spot, and assuming that alone didn't take me years, how do I know it won't have been looted by thieves hundreds or even thousands of years ago?"

"As you said, the chamber you discovered the second one in was well hidden. Perhaps it is the same with this one." Dr. Reid suddenly tilted his head to the side as if trying to listen to something faint in the distance. Tex had seen the look on his face before and knew not to interrupt while the professor was putting the puzzle pieces together in his head.

"Or maybe it *was* that way," Reid said at last.

"What do you mean?

"What if a conqueror already found the third Tear and it's no longer in Egypt?"

"Then it could be anywhere in the world and we're worse off than if it was somewhere in Giza."

"Not necessarily."

The cat sat up abruptly and hissed. Reid pressed a finger to his lips. A few seconds later a woman walked briskly into view, books clutched tight against her chest. It was the same librarian that had interrupted their conversation a couple weeks before. She glowered at the cat, put away three books on a shelf, and then left.

"That cursed woman is going to be the death of me," Dr. Reid muttered.

Tex laughed. "Then how come I think it's actually going to be you that's the death of her?"

"Because you are a student of human nature."

"Not really, but the cat hates her so I figure sooner or later she has to go," he joked.

The cat laid back down, but kept his watchful eyes fixed on the place where the librarian had disappeared.

"I should explain," Dr. Reid said as he stroked his cat's back.

"That would be helpful."

"I believe the Tear might have rested in the Great Pyramid."

Tex shook his head. "That place is empty. If it ever was there it would have been stolen a long, long time ago."

"It's not entirely empty," the professor said. "You are forgetting the coffin in the king's chamber."

"The hollowed out hunk of rock with no lid and nothing inside?" Tex asked skeptically.

"The same. You know there have been rumors that the coffin itself originated in Atlantis."

Tex realized he had leaned forward, eager to hear more. "What do the legends say?"

"Nothing more than that, unfortunately. However, if it is from Atlantis, it would stand to reason that the Tear of Man could have been there as well."

"Okay, but again we run into the missing for thousands of years problem."

"Not if the part about a conqueror was accurate and actually meant something."

Tex stared at him for a few seconds before answering. "You mean you think the Tear would magically reveal itself if the right person came along?"

"Well maybe not magically, but maybe there is something in a certain personality type that would allow them to view the room differently than a normal man and it would help them to find the Tear. Like how you were able to find that hidden tomb in the Grand Canyon that others missed."

"Yeah, but I knew I was looking for something like that."

"Maybe a conqueror entered the Great Pyramid also aware that they were looking for something."

"As it turned out I needed the first Tear to open the door for the second one. It was also weird because when I inserted the Tear in the space for it on the wall it glowed red hot and that's when the words became visible."

Dr. Reid cocked his head to the side. "Have you encountered anything before now other than human contact that made the Tears glow?"

"No, nothing else."

"Interesting. Perhaps we're not dealing with magic so much as very advanced technology."

"Maybe. Given that I needed the first Tear to recover the second you think someone could have obtained the third without the other two?"

"There definitely seems to have been an intended order in which these were found starting in the west and moving east. Since you did not have to do anything special to collect the first Tear, though, it is possible that the key to the third one has nothing to do with the other two."

"But getting the third one requires a different perspective or mind-set."

"Precisely, ensuring that not just anyone could collect all three."

Tex felt a headache coming on and he pressed his fingers to his temples. "Okay, let's assume that you're right and that someone may have already removed the third Tear from the pyramid. That leaves us with figuring out who and where it could be now."

"Correct."

"Okay, let's think. I've heard an old legend that Alexander the Great was inside. He definitely had that conqueror mindset."

"I've heard that, too, though I'm not sure of its veracity. I do know there was another conqueror who was supposed to have spent some time inside the king's chamber in the great pyramid and been deeply affected by what happened to him there."

"Who?" Tex asked, curiosity roaring through him.

"Napoleon."

"Really?"

"That's the story. Apparently after spending time alone in the king's chamber, he emerged, visibly shaken. He refused to tell the others with him what he'd seen. On his death bed a friend asked him and he almost told him but then thought better of it saying the man would never believe him anyway."

"You think whatever happened to him in the pyramid resulted in him taking possession of the Tear?"

"I would say that it's certainly worth serious consideration."

"Okay, assuming for a moment that he did take it. Where on earth would it be now?" Tex asked.

"Something that precious, if he had any inkling what it was, he would keep it close at hand."

Tex thought of the two Tears that right now were nestled in his inner jacket pocket. He would never risk leaving them alone somewhere.

Dr. Reid starting nodding his head. "I think I have an idea. Give me a minute."

Dr. Reid got up, grabbed his walking stick, and headed off at a brisker pace than Tex had ever seen him walk. He was gone two minutes and when he returned he was carrying a large volume under his arm.

As soon as he had sat back down he placed the volume on the desk and flipped through it. He stopped on a page with a picture of Napoleon and after a moment pulled a small magnifying glass out of one of his pockets. He peered closely at the page and then straightened with a look of triumph.

He passed both book and magnifying glass over to Tex who took them reluctantly. The picture in question was a drawing of Napoleon after he had died and was prepared for burial. Tex stared at it through the magnifying glass and froze while staring at the ribbons and medals pinned on his chest. A stone in the middle of one of them looked very familiar.

He looked up at Dr. Reid who was grinning from ear-to-ear.

"So, Napoleon found the Tear in the pyramid," Tex said quietly.

"I would say so."

"And you were right, he kept it close to him."

"As you no doubt are keeping yours close."

Tex barely restrained himself from putting a hand over the pocket they were in. Sometimes he did that just to ensure that they were still there. It was becoming an obsessive habit, one that did not sit well with him. The sooner this entire thing was over the better for his peace of mind.

Of course, this was a wrinkle that was designed to cost him headaches, and for a moment he thought about giving up. The urge to hand Dr. Reid the two Tears, stand up and walk away was almost overwhelming. Maybe the stress of carrying them was to be expected. Maybe that was why only a conqueror could claim the third, someone who was willing to go to extraordinary lengths.

After a minute he cleared his throat. "Do you have any contacts in France?"

"None that could help with something like this. At least, none that I would trust to help. And any request through official channels, well, it could take years and they would want to know why."

"At which point they'd either dismiss us as crazy or decide to find the Tear for themselves," Tex said.

"My thoughts exactly."

"This is far more trouble than I'm prepared for," Tex admitted. "You know me, I'll go just about anywhere and do just about anything. But what you're suggesting...it's crossing a line even for me."

"I know, but it's important. Atlantis. Who knows when there will be another chance to discover it and find out its secrets?"

"This is going to cost more than I have."

"I can help with that?"

"On a professor's salary?" Tex asked, raising an eyebrow.

"I have a little saved up, and it would be worth it to me. I'll fund your expedition."

Tex let out a short laugh. "That's a polite word for a rather ugly business."

"Most archaeologists don't enjoy being called grave robbers in my experience."

"And I'm one of them, but this? This is theft, pure and simple."

Tex groaned to himself as he stared again at the picture. The tear-shaped drop was unmistakable. It looked just like the two he already had, and that meant just one thing. "I'm going to have to break into Napoleon's tomb."

Chapter 15

Tex leaned back in his chair, overwhelmed by the prospect. "Isn't Napoleon buried inside of something like six coffins?"

"Yes, getting to the body will not be easy."

"You're telling me. I've got a suggestion, why don't you go after this one while I stay here and study the tablet to figure out what we do next?"

Dr. Reid smiled. "Would that we could do things that way."

Tex glanced at the walking stick that was once more propped up against the table. "You said a couple minutes ago that your rafting accident wasn't an accident. Do you know who attacked you?"

"No, unfortunately I do not," Dr. Reid said.

"I keep wondering if it was one of the men with the Helenium flower card."

The other man shook his head. "If it was, I wouldn't know."

"You know, you could still make it there someday," Tex said, trying to address what had to be a painful loss to the other man.

"Even if I had made it before, from what you've said it would have been futile without already having a Tear in my possession."

"Yes, but there's so much else there that you'd love to see and needs to be catalogued by someone like you."

Dr. Reid shook his head. "Maybe someday," he said, sorrow tingeing his voice. "But today, our focus must be on getting you to Paris or this whole thing will have been for naught."

"Before I go I would like to take a look at the tablet. Maybe we can figure out what comes next. I know the three Tears have to be together, but beyond that, I don't know what to do."

"See it you shall," Dr. Reid said, with an air of having made up his mind about something. "Go home and get packed. I'll be by late tonight with the tablet after I've made your travel arrangements."

"Are you sure?" Tex asked.

"Yes, there's no time to waste."

The sudden urgency in Dr. Reid's voice drove Tex to his feet. "I'll see you tonight."

The other man nodded, but he was gazing far off, clearly lost deep in his own thoughts. Tex hurried from the library. It sounded like the professor would have him leaving the following day which meant he had precious little time to lose.

On his way out he turned, wanting to take one last look at the wastepaper basket. He was curious if the papers that had been burning in there were just random trash that people had thrown out or if they actually had some significance.

The basket was gone, though. The firemen had probably disposed of it. He mentally upbraided himself for not thinking to check yesterday. There was nothing he could do about it now.

He left the library. He had some shopping to do before he could go home and pack. His first stop was at the haberdasher where he usually bought his clothes and, more frequently, his hats.

The proprietor, and older gentleman with silver hair, hailed his entrance with a smile and a warm greeting. "Let me guess, a new hat for a new adventure?"

"Unfortunately, you're right," Tex admitted.

The old man's eyes sparkled. "You know, I think this store could stay open solely on the strength of your need for hats."

"I don't doubt it."

"Honestly, I don't know how you manage to lose so many. If you were a motion picture hero you'd have been dead many times already."

"Sometimes I feel like I am," Tex said with a smile.

It was true. In motion pictures a man only lost his hat if he was dead or about to die. Fortunately Tex didn't suffer from any superstitions regarding hat loss. Otherwise he'd be in serious trouble.

The door opened and another man came in. His coat was a bit shabby and his slacks a little worn at the knees. Clearly he was in need of a new wardrobe. He began to browse as the owner led Tex over to a wall adorned with hats.

"Now, do you want the same hat as last time or are you feeling more adventurous today?"

"You ask me that every time," Tex commented.

"And one of these days you'll humor me and tell me you're feeling adventurous," the old man said with a twinkle in his eye.

"I have enough adventure in my life that I don't need to find it in my choice of headwear."

"Of course, you're probably right, but one of these days I'd like to see you in a nice bowler. Of course, one of these days you'll find a nice girl and settle down. Then the most adventurous choice you'll make is to wear a top hat at your wedding," he chortled.

Tex didn't say anything and the old man got down a hat in his style and size. The fact that he didn't need to ask the size was just sad, a testament to how many hats Tex had bought in the place.

"Now, can I sell you something that isn't a hat?"

"Not today," Tex said with a smile.

"Can't blame a fellow for trying."

They moved over to the counter. Tex pulled out his wallet, and out of the corner of his eye noticed that the other customer in the store was going through a rack of jackets, but he wasn't looking at any of them. Instead he was watching Tex.

That couldn't be a good thing.

Tex paid for the hat and waved off the hatbox, opting instead to just wear it. He needed to pick up some other things and a hatbox was the last thing he needed to be carrying around. Especially if the man who was staring at him was going to try something.

After having paid Tex settled the hat on his head. He leaned across the counter and dropped his voice low. "The other gentleman, a customer of yours?"

"I've never seen him before."

Tex had been afraid of that. "Thanks," he said, straightening up.

"Now, try and keep this hat on your head," the owner joked.

Tex smiled. "The day I manage that will be the day I'm really in trouble."

He turned and left the shop, walking close by the man who was watching him. Tex turned to look at him, but the man averted his eyes.

Outside on the street Tex began walking slowly toward his next stop, keeping his eyes on the windows of the stores he passed. Sure enough he hadn't gone very far when he could see the other man exit the store and begin to follow him.

Tex never carried his gun or knife with him when he was home. He was beginning to regret that decision. The other man kept a certain distance behind him, stopping when he stopped, speeding up when he did.

There was no doubt that the man was following him. He just needed to figure out why. Also, what was the man waiting for?

Finally Tex turned at one of the corners. Once he had he stopped, waiting just out of sight. When the man came around the corner Tex grabbed his arm and threw him up against the wall of the building and pinned him there with his hand around his throat.

"Who are you?" Tex demanded.

The man flailed at him, futilely trying to pull Tex's fingers away from his throat.

"I'm nobody," he managed to gasp.

"You're going to be nobody if you don't tell me why you've been following me," Tex warned, squeezing a little tighter.

The man began to choke. “I’m not following you!” he wheezed.

“Wrong answer. You get one more and then that’s it,” Tex warned, putting a fraction more pressure.

The man’s eyes were starting to bug out of his head. Tex kept watching for him to make a move to draw a weapon, but he didn’t.

“Now, one last time who sent you?”

The man was gurgling now, unable to speak. Tex relaxed his hold slightly. “A man, I never met him before.”

“A man you never met before told you to follow me?”

“That’s right.”

“Why?”

“I don’t know. He just told me that he’d pay me to follow you. He gave me ten dollars in advance and said he’d give me more after.”

“And you didn’t ask him why?”

“No. He didn’t seem the kind you’d ask questions of.”

“What did he look like?”

“He was standing in an alley, his face was all in darkness.”

“And all he wanted you to do was follow me?” Tex asked incredulously. “Were you supposed to tell him where I went and what I was doing?”

“I don’t know, he never said.”

“Where were you supposed to meet him to collect the rest of your money?”

“He said he’d find me.”

The man was completely unhelpful, and it baffled Tex. It didn’t seem like a good plan. If someone wanted information they would have asked him to give it to them.

If someone wanted to attack him, they would have paid the man to do that.

"Just follow. There's nothing else, you're positively sure?"

"There was just one other thing. I told him it wouldn't be important."

"What was it?"

"He told me to tell you something if I got caught, but I told him that I was sly and you'd never catch me. He didn't seem to be worried about it."

Now they were getting somewhere. The man wasn't anywhere even close to sly and whoever had hired him had been relying on that. So, this wasn't about following him or hurting him or stealing from him. It was about sending a message.

"What is the message he told you to give me?" Tex asked.

"He told me to tell you not to go to Paris."

Tex stepped back and let go of the other man who sagged against the building and gasped in great gulps of air. "That's it?" Tex asked.

The other man nodded.

"If you ever follow me again, it will be the last thing you do, you understand?"

The man nodded again and the fear in his eyes was real.

Someone didn't want him to go to Paris. How was that even possible when only he and Dr. Reid knew that was where he was headed? Was it possible that someone else knew all about the Tears, including their location, and was trying to warn him off for some reason?

Things were getting stranger by the minute and he didn't like being this out of control. Was this mysterious man the same one who Lena worked for? After all, she'd insisted that he wanted Tex off his current quest as much as he wanted the gemstone.

Having caught his breath the man ran off and Tex barely paid attention. There were too many players and he still didn't know who half of them were. There was one thing he did know for certain. Warning or no warning, he was going to Paris. Nothing could stop him from doing that now.

A couple of hours later Tex returned home in possession of a few new tools in addition to his fine new hat. The rest of his shopping had been uneventful even though he'd constantly been looking over his shoulder. When he walked in the house Fuzzyboots greeted him impatiently at the door with a meow that sounded like he was actually scolding him.

"I forgot about you," Tex admitted to the cat. "I'm used to being able to just leave at a moment's notice when I'm not teaching."

If anything the meow the cat responded with sounded even more cross.

Tex shook his head. He was going to end up as crazy as Dr. Reid was when it came to his cat.

He packed his bags, including a new suitcase he'd had to break down and buy since he kept losing those as well as hats. He was taking far more with him than he normally would, but there were some purchases he didn't need to be making in Paris as they would be likely to raise eyebrows.

He hadn't been finished more than fifteen minutes when the doorbell rang. He went to open the door and found Dr. Reid and his cat both standing on the porch.

"Come in," Tex said, standing aside.

The cat walked in first, his tail high in the air, looking for all the world like he was the scout for an army regiment checking the area before his human walked in.

Dr. Reid stepped in a moment later. He had a large parcel in his one arm and was leaning heavily on his walking stick.

Tex closed the door and led the way into the living room where Fuzzyboots looked up from where he was lounging on the couch. A moment later Fuzzyboots noticed Dr. Reid's cat and jumped down. The two felines approached each other cautiously, but then after a moment rubbed heads.

"Beautiful cat," Dr. Reid commented as he set down his parcel and pulled off the trench coat he was wearing and folded it over the arm of the couch.

"Thanks, although I don't know what I'm going to do with him while I'm gone."

"That's simple. He'll stay with us until you get back," Dr. Reid said as if it was the most natural thing in the world.

"Thanks, I'd appreciate that."

Tex sat down on a chair. "Today someone followed me after I left the library. He claimed someone he didn't know hired him to do that and to give me a message when I caught him."

"What was the message?" Dr. Reid asked.

"Don't go to Paris."

"How on earth did someone know that was where you are heading?"

"You tell me."

"I don't have the faintest idea."

"Maybe the library isn't as secure a location as you think it is. Maybe that nosy librarian your cat hates has been spying on you."

Dr. Reid narrowed his eyes. "I wouldn't put it past her," he said. "Horrid woman."

"Someone knows, at any rate."

"You're not going to listen, are you?"

"No, wild horses couldn't keep me away from Paris now. I don't like warnings or threats, they tend to make me want to do the opposite."

"Good. Now that that's settled, let's get on with it."

Dr. Reid reached out to the parcel and unwrapped it from the plain brown paper that was currently secured around it. At last he pulled free a stone that was about eighteen inches tall and twelve inches wide. Remarkably it was less than half an inch thick. He handed it to Tex who could see that it was covered in miniscule hieroglyphs.

"This is incredible," Tex said. "It looks like it was cut with some sort of modern machinery. It's so smooth on both sides. And it's thin, way too thin. And the lettering is too small, too fine. This can't be that old."

"And yet, it is."

"How is this even possible?" Tex asked.

"Hopefully when we find Atlantis we will have the answer to that," Dr. Reid said.

Tex carefully set it down and went to retrieve a magnifying glass which he then brought to bear on the hieroglyphs. They were stunning in their absolute clarity as he was able to clearly see them with the help of the magnification. When he finally put down the magnifying glass and looked up again at Dr. Reid he just shook his head.

"I don't know what to say."

"The world is full of mysteries, Charles. This is just one of them," Dr. Reid said with a knowing smile.

Tex was staggered. The technology to create something like this barely existed in the modern world.

"How do we know this is a legitimate artifact, and not some hoax?" Tex asked.

"Because the provenance on that piece actually goes back to the time of Christ. It's been handed down carefully, documented. It was only with a great many personal assurances that I was able to wrest it away from its current keeper. This piece is priceless, not just because it speaks of Atlantis, but because of its age and the skill and craftsmanship employed to make it. Nothing like it is sitting in any museums of the world."

"This piece alone could upset our current theories about the ancient world," Tex mused.

"Yes, but far better to use it to find a much greater, more revealing treasure, no?"

"You're right. It's just staggering, that's all."

"I have decided to let you take it with you to Paris."

Tex glanced up sharply. "You know where I'm going, what I'm doing. There's a high risk that I'll be caught. Why risk sending this there with me?"

"Because I believe in you. I believe that you will succeed. And I believe that when you do you will need this to tell you what to do next."

"I can come home and we can figure that out together once I have the third Tear."

"I'm afraid we won't have that much time on our side," Dr. Reid said. "I believe that when you have all three Tears you will need to act quickly in using them to discover the location of the lost city."

Tex could feel that scratching again at the back of his mind, the one that urged him to hurry and also warned him of danger.

"Why do I get the feeling that there's some sort of countdown?" he asked.

"Because I believe there is."

Dr. Reid pulled a few sheets of paper out of the pocket of his trench coat and handed them to Tex. "Someone else began to translate the stone. It's rough, very rough in a few places and there are some things they haven't been able to decipher at all. However, in reading this over it seems to mention that there are only three times in history in which the continent can be found."

Dr. Reid cleared his throat before saying the words that sent chills up and down Tex's spine.

"Found and raised."

Chapter 16

"What did you say?" Tex asked slowly.

Dr. Reid smiled. "You heard me correctly."

"Raised, how is that even possible? They can't even raise sunken ships, how on earth could someone raise an entire island?"

"I trust that once all the Tears are in your possession that will be made clear."

Tex sat for a moment, not even looking at the papers in his hands. The enormity of it all was getting to him. "This could change the entire world," he finally said.

"It certainly would," Dr. Reid affirmed.

That knowledge weighed him down as though it were a burden he had to bear. The world would be changed for better or worse and he would be responsible.

"This might take longer than I previously thought," he said.

"If you're worried about your classes starting in the fall, don't be. I'll cover for you if you can't be there."

"It's not just that," Tex said, struggling to put into words what he was feeling.

Dr. Reid reached out and put a hand on his shoulder. "Feeling the weight of the world, are we?"

"Yeah, to put it mildly."

"I understand. It is a terrible burden, but I think it's time the world knew the truth."

"I wish I was as sure as you are that the world's ready for that much truth," Tex said, shaking his head.

Dr. Reid smiled grimly. "Well, we'll find out."

Tex shook himself, trying to focus back on the task at hand. "When do I leave for Paris?"

"Tomorrow," Dr. Reid said, handing him an envelope. "I secured you passage on a cargo ship, I hope that's alright."

"It's fine by me. There'll only be a handful of other people to deal with, and we should make good time."

"My thoughts exactly. I've made a hotel reservation for you. Inside the envelope is enough money to pay for your hotel, food, passage back, and, hopefully, anything else that comes up."

"I appreciate it," Tex said. He felt bad about taking the other man's money, but reminded himself that he really was going on this quest more for Dr. Reid than himself. And, if they found Atlantis, there was the very real possibility that they'd both end up wealthy men.

"I should leave you to rest before your journey," the professor said, standing abruptly. He glanced over at the cats. "What have you called yours?" he asked.

"Oh, Fuzzyboots."

"Fuzzyboots?" Dr. Reid asked in surprise.

"That's what it looks like he's wearing on his back legs," Tex said.

Dr. Reid sighed. "Very well, come on, Fuzzyboots, you're with us."

He headed for the door.

"You're probably going to have to pick him up," Tex said. To his surprise, though, both cats turned and walked after Dr. Reid.

He got up and followed them to the door.

"Good luck, Charles," Dr. Reid said.

"Thank you."

He opened the door and the professor walked into the darkness, the two cats walking beside him.

While it was still dark out Tex arrived at the dock that the ship he would be on was leaving from. He had taken every precaution as he left home to make sure he wasn't being followed. He couldn't shake the feeling that Lena would show up at any moment to spoil things and keep him from getting on the boat.

No one seemed to follow him on his way there and at the dock itself he only encountered sailors, many of whom regarded him with suspicion. He knew that he stood out wearing nice slacks and his tweed coat. Professors didn't usually make it down to the docks let alone book passage on a cargo ship. The loose coat allowed him to wear his shoulder holster with his Colt M1911 in it with no one being any the wiser. The last thing that he wanted to advertise was that he was a man looking for trouble, a man with something worth stealing. Hence he dressed as he did instead of wearing his khakis and his gun belt. All of those were packed in his luggage along with his Colt 45.

The captain seemed like a pleasant man and personally escorted Tex to the room he would be staying in for the voyage. It was not unusual for ships to take on a handful of passengers for such a voyage. It was a cheaper way of going for the person who didn't care about the journey just the destination.

"Will you be carrying other passengers?" Tex asked before the captain took his leave.

"Only a couple this crossing. You're actually the last to arrive," the captain told him.

He hoped that meant that the other two passengers had nothing to do with him. He figured he'd find out more at dinner.

Once the captain left he settled into his cabin and within the hour they were underway. Tex breathed a little easier once they hit the open ocean. He got out a few books he had brought for research. The tablet and its translation were sealed in a hidden compartment in the bottom of his suitcase and as much as he wanted to study them he felt it best they remain there for the duration of the voyage. He set about reading up on the tomb of Napoleon instead.

That night at dinner Tex's fears were somewhat allayed when he was introduced to the other two passengers. Both were men traveling alone. One was a penny-pinching businessman who was on his way to France to make a deal and the other was an older gentleman who was going to France to visit his son who had married a girl over there during the war and had stayed. Neither of them seemed even remotely interested in him which made Tex happy. It was a good thing, too. They would be on the ship together for several days and the last thing Tex wanted was to constantly be watching his back. Instead he could devote his time to learning everything else he could about Napoleon's tomb and the legends of Atlantis.

A little over two weeks later Tex was standing, staring at Napoleon's tomb, stunned that his luck had held out so far. The ocean passage had been blessedly uneventful which had given him plenty of time to reflect on just how much of an idiot he was for even attempting this.

He had been in the city for a few days now and he had studied Napoleon's tomb inside the Eglise du Dome Church at the Hotel des Invalides from every angle. He had the tools he needed and it was time to put his mad plan into action.

Just for fun he had actually gone through the motions and checked out of his hotel earlier that day. All of his stuff he had put in a car that he had rented.

He had left his getaway car parked several blocks away where it wasn't likely to be found until morning. On the passenger seat he had left a package addressed to Dr. Reid and with proper postage. Inside were the tablet, its translation, and the two Tears he had already collected. If he failed in his mission there was a slim chance that some kindly soul would send the package on. It was a fool's hope, but it was better than being caught with the items on him.

It was just after midnight. Breaking into the church had been the easy part. He had already subdued the lone night watchman and could be guaranteed privacy for a while at least. Yet now that he was standing in front of Napoleon's resting place he was more convinced than ever that he had gone insane. There was no way he wasn't going to get caught. He had to prepare for that.

The tomb was actually the third resting place of the emperor. Tex kept hoping that in all the moving of the body something hadn't happened to the Tear. He didn't want to go through everything he was about to go through for nothing.

Napoleon's coffin was under a dome on top of a pedestal made of green granite. What made the task ahead especially daunting was that it was actually six coffins nested inside of each other with his body in the innermost coffin like some sort of macabre Russian nesting doll. The outer coffin was made out of red porphyry which was granite from Egypt that had been highly prized in antiquity partially for its hardness and had been often formed into monuments. The material had only been mined from one area in Egypt and production had stopped in the 4th century A.D. and the mine had been lost.

Napoleon himself had the scientific members of his expedition search Egypt for the mine in vain. The mine had finally been rediscovered two years after his death. It was the ultimate irony that the stone he had sought in life finally became his in death. In addition to that coffin there were also coffins of ebony, mahogany, iron, and two made up of lead.

Ebony was a dense black wood. The name ebony was derived from the Egyptian word for the name and the wood had been used in ancient Egyptian tombs and often carved with hieroglyphs. Two of the six coffins had a strong Egyptian connection, and even though he knew Napoleon hadn't chosen the materials himself, it still seemed like a sign of his connection with the Tear that he had found hidden in that country.

With Tex he had crowbars, a drill, and several other instruments. From a maintenance closet he had taken a ladder to make getting access to the top of the monument easier. He desperately hoped that some of the inner coffins would have lids that were easier to remove.

I am not a grave robber, he repeated mentally to himself as he picked up the first tool.

The work was agonizingly slow and difficult. As he bypassed each layer he would stop to wipe the accumulated sweat off his face. The sweat was the result of fear as much as it was exertion. He had to pause to take a short rest right before tackling the final coffin lid.

He was sitting with his back to one of the twelve pillars of victory that surrounded the coffins. He couldn't help but feel that in having his grave desecrated and the Tear stolen from him Napoleon would once more be experiencing a defeat. It was no fun to best a dead man, though.

"I am not a grave robber," Tex muttered to himself as he stood up and prepared to finish the job.

Fifteen minutes later he was face-to-face with a conqueror. Tex held his breath as he looked to see if the Tear was still where it had been in the sketching. For a moment he didn't see it and his heart began to pound. He couldn't have gone through all of this for nothing only to find out the Tear had been lost in all the times the body had been moved. The Tear could even have been stolen.

Then he pushed aside one of the other medals and he saw it. Relief flooded through him. Using a small jewelers tool he had brought he pried the Tear out of its setting. As he lifted it free he couldn't help but feel a quick flush of guilt.

I am a grave robber.

He forced the thought from his mind as the Tear began to heat up. He quickly concealed the Tear inside a small, hidden compartment in the key ring he was carrying. It was a precaution he had opted to take in case he was caught after finding the Tear.

He climbed down off the ladder. His gear was scattered around on the floor, and he quickly grabbed what he needed. The crowbars, drill, and one or two other large items he decided to leave behind. Carrying them on the streets even for a short while at this point would be dangerous and there was nothing about any of them that could trace back to him.

For one insane moment he had the urge to take a small piece of the red porphyry lid with him. He pushed the thought from his mind, though. Only people who wanted to get caught took trophies like that. He most certainly never wanted his name linked with this.

He walked quickly through the building, heading for the door that he had come in through. He cast a glance toward the room that he had left the unconscious guard tied up in and suddenly froze.

The man was missing.

Chapter 17

Tex began to run, heading for the exit as fast as he could. How had the guard gotten loose? Had a different guard come in and found him? He was surprised that once the guard was free, however it had happened, he hadn't come looking for Tex. Maybe he was too busy calling the police. Either way he had to get out of there now.

He could see the door he was going to exit through now. Suddenly a bright light shone in his eyes and he heard a voice shouting in French. He threw his arm up over his eyes, struggling to make out anything beyond the light from the flashlight.

"Who are you?" someone demanded in French.

"Napoleon," he answered. He had to try for convincing them he was crazy. It might buy him a little extra time. Who knew, they might even believe it. After all, only someone who was completely crazy would have broken into Napoleon's tomb in the first place.

There was a flurry of French that followed his declaration, all of it too fast and too agitated for him to understand. He heard running steps approaching. He had at least two captors.

The two spoke to each other rapidly and he wished he knew what they were saying. His French was too rusty, though. After a few seconds the flashlight dipped toward the ground slightly and he was able to make out two men, one of them the guard he had tied up.

The more the two of them talked the less they were looking at him. Tex waited, knowing he'd likely have one moment to act when the time came. He watched them intently. It was clear that the guard he had tied up had discovered what he'd done to Napoleon's tomb. He could only imagine they were debating whether or not to let the firing squad handle him or if they should just shoot him now and get it over with.

The flashlight dipped farther toward the floor.

Outside the building he heard the distinctive sound of a siren. The other men heard it, too, turning slightly toward the sound.

It was the opening Tex needed. He lunged forward, snatching the flashlight from the one guard's hand and hitting him in the head with it before he could react.

The other man had his gun halfway out of its holster when Tex hit him with the flashlight, catching him on the jaw.

Both men slumped to the ground unconscious and Tex bolted for the door as loud banging began to reverberate through the building. He still had his bag with him. It was a black duffel he had brought just for the occasion. None of his normal field kit was in it nor did it hold anything of sentimental value. He couldn't risk hitting the streets with it so he dropped it between the two guards and ran for the exit.

Outside he closed the door behind him quietly and crept down the side of the building, heart in his throat. He took a glance out front and saw that there were two police cars already present and another four were pulling up. Officers began pouring into the building, guns drawn.

He had been worried about making it out of the country with the Tear. He was starting to think that he should have worried about making it out of the country with his life.

He turned and walked away from the building as quickly as he could. He was going in the opposite direction to the one he needed to go to get his car. He was just going to have to find a way to circle around.

He turned down an alley between two buildings, staring over his shoulder until he had traversed half of it.

A sailor who had imbibed too much was passed out in the alley, a half drunk bottle of scotch still clutched in his hand. Tex pressed himself against the one wall where he'd be hidden in shadow from anyone on the street a few feet away.

Everywhere he could hear running feet. His first instinct was to find a place to hide and lie low for a few hours. That plan wouldn't work though. Every minute he left the car unattended was another minute where the other two Tears and the tablet could be discovered and stolen. Plus for a crime of this magnitude they might block access out of the city soon. Before they could organize that he had to be long gone. And that meant heading out into the street which was the last place he wanted to go.

He ditched his black sweater. His white undershirt was generic and not the color clothing they'd be looking for. He took the unconscious man's bottle from his hand. Tex liberally doused himself with the scotch so that he reeked of alcohol. Next he borrowed the man's hat. The sailor would likely get in trouble for losing it, but it would be nothing compared to what waited Tex if he was caught.

Heart in his throat, Tex staggered out onto the street. He stumble walked as quickly as he felt he could without arousing suspicion. Ahead of him he saw a police officer running in his direction. Tex began to sing to himself, slurring his words liberally. He tensed as the gap between himself and the officer narrowed. The moment of truth was nearly upon him.

The police officer rushed by without giving him even a single look. *One down, hundreds more to go*, he thought grimly. In truth he had no idea how many officers might be standing between him and the car. He just hoped they were all as easily fooled.

He kept going, weaving as he put one foot in front of the other. He dare not look behind him even though the skin on the back of his neck was prickling as though he were being stared at. He had to keep going, trusting that if there was someone watching him they, too, would soon be convinced he was nothing more than a drunken sailor.

A minute later he heard the sound of running footsteps behind him. His muscles coiled, ready to leap into action. He could try and outrun them and make it to the car or he could turn to fight, hoping to take them by surprise. Either move would most certainly give him away and bring more officers down upon him.

Why didn't those who were running up behind him say anything? They should be shouting for him to stop. They weren't though. He took a deep breath and forced himself to keep walking while he began to sing even louder. He had to trust in his disguise.

Moments later two officers ran past him and kept going down the street. At the intersection they continued going straight which was a relief to him since he would be turning left to reach his car.

He kept going, heart in his throat, singing as if he didn't have a care in the world. He had to make a couple more turns before he was heading toward his car.

He put his hand in his pocket, checking that the keys for the car were still there as was the customized keychain that concealed the latest Tear. He saw more police running by and panic kept edging up in him.

He had to make it to his car, though. At this rate they would have sealed off the roads leading out of the city by the time he got to them. He was close, less than a block away. He grit his teeth and kept going.

At the intersection he turned, struggling to keep himself from breaking into a run. He could see his car just half a block ahead and was grateful that no one was lurking around it. He pulled his keys out of his pocket as he prepared to cross the street.

He stepped off the curb, made it half a dozen steps, and something slammed into him sending him sprawling to the ground. Tex watched in horror as his keys flew out of his hand and skidded across the street. The Tear was in that keychain. He had to get it back. He pushed off the ground, starting to scramble to his feet when he was kicked in the ribs.

He flipped onto his back and saw his assailant, a huge mountain of a man who looked more Polynesian than French. Before he could kick him again, Tex slammed his fist into the inside of the man's knee. The man collapsed with a scream of anguish that was probably heard for blocks. Tex leaped to his feet, grabbed the big man's right arm, stretched it tight, and kicked him in the armpit. The other man's shoulder dislocated and before he could even respond Tex threw his entire weight onto the shoulder, shattering it.

He let go of the man and ran for the car, scooping up his keys in the process. Just as he was unlocking the car he heard a commotion at the end of the street and people screaming at him in French to halt.

Tex threw himself inside the car, started it, and hit the gas. A bullet shattered the rear window and another whizzed past his ear.

Tex hunched low over the steering wheel and skidded into a right turn at the next intersection, tires screaming in anguish. For a moment he thought they were going to lose their grip on the road and panic flared through him. The car straightened out, though, and he hit the gas again, swerving around a car that was in front of him.

He made three more quick turns, hoping it would be enough to throw the police off his trail. Then he forced himself to slow down. Speeding would only draw attention to himself and he could end up with more officers pursuing him for that, not even realizing their fellow officers were searching for him for something far worse.

It felt like a lifetime passed but he was finally almost out of the city and on the open roads. Then right in front of him he saw a roadblock. Police had a barricade set up across the road and cars parked on either side. He slowed, wondering if there was another way out of the city that wouldn't be blocked. A policeman saw him slowing and waved him forward. He turned and spoke to another officer whose hand went to the gun on his waist.

This was it, Tex realized. He was trapped.

Chapter 18

Tex stared at the barricade. There was no way around it. If he turned around and made a run for it the officers would pursue. And once they had seen the car he was driving they could share that information with police all over the country.

He was out of options and out of time. He wondered if there was any way he could take out both officers. Maybe if he kept up the drunken sailor act they'd arrest him for that never realizing that he was the man everyone else was after.

Suddenly a car swerved around him. He glanced over, wondering who was driving so insanely. From the driver's seat Lena smiled and blew him a kiss before cutting him off. He watched, stunned, as she purposely rammed one of the police cars.

All the officers ran toward her, guns drawn, and all that was left between him and freedom was a wooden barricade. He hit the gas and a moment later he was blasting through it.

Lena would be fine. She wasn't the one the police were after and she'd play some helpless female role and they'd probably fall over themselves trying to be helpful. He had no idea why she'd done that, but he just pressed down harder on the gas and kept going.

Tex drove for hours and finally made it into Belgium. He breathed easier once he had crossed the border. He made it to Brussels as the sun was rising. Once there he stopped at a hotel, surprising the man at the front desk who quickly gave him a room. Tex carried everything upstairs to his room and locked the door.

He was still wide awake, the adrenalin only slowly fading away. He sat down at the table in his hotel room where he very carefully unwrapped the package he had addressed to Dr. Reid. He laid out the two Tears on the table and then retrieved the third from his keychain and laid it on the table as well. Together these three were supposed to help him find the lost civilization of Atlantis. The only question was, how?

The three Tears remained passive. He had half expected that when all three were together that something would happen, even if it just meant that they started to all glow together.

Using a pen he nudged them together until they were all touching. Still nothing.

With a sigh he turned to the piece of tablet he had and the translation. The tablet he placed on the table. He also retrieved his magnifying glass so he could read the fine inscription. It still boggled his mind that such work was done in antiquity.

He got out his journal and a pencil and prepared to copy the translation, making changes where they needed to be made. Finally he picked up the pieces of paper with the translation. Dr. Reid had warned him that it was very rough. Neither of them had had a chance to study the tablet yet in detail. Hopefully a very rough translation was all that he would need. He perused it carefully, noting that in places the translator had put question marks where he was potentially unsure of the translation and making other notations in parenthesis.

> Atlantis the mighty island (?) has fallen, sunk below the waves by a vengeful creature. The parent of all great lands (?) that are and that will be is collected long.

Collected long? What on earth was that supposed to mean? Tex reread the sentence but the ending still didn't make sense. He would have to come back to it later after he finished reading the whole thing. The question marks also troubled Tex as they represented the parts the translator thought it possible they were getting wrong. Yet no such question mark followed *collected long*.

> Its (I don't know what the next word means) are lost at the bottom of the sea. There it need not stay long (?) Portals will open that recovery may be made. Once they close all is lost forever. The watery grave is marked below instead of above. The Tears of Man show the way to the grave and must be gathered together. Where the priests tell the stories still the (I don't know what the next word means) column may be found which will bring a light to everything and show the truth. One Tear lost beyond the seas. One Tear carried by a pharaoh to a new land. One Tear may only by the second be found.

It felt rough and he didn't like the question marks or the indication that there were words the man hadn't been able to translate. With a sigh Tex picked up the magnifying glass and began to examine the tablet for himself. Slowly he began to write in his journal, working until he was beyond tired. It had to be finished, though. He couldn't rely on the original translation either. The phrase "collected long" that had seemed so strange to him actually should have been translated as "remembered forever".

It took a while, but finally he had recorded the last word. He sat back and rubbed his eyes for a moment before picking up his journal and reading the entire thing through with the new translation.

> Atlantis the mighty continent has been struck down, sunk below the waves by a vengeful god. The mother of all great civilizations that are and that will be is remembered forever. Its technologies are lost at the bottom of the sea. There it need not abide forever. Windows of opportunity exist to restore what was lost. Once they close all is lost forever. The watery grave is marked below instead of above. Three Tears of Man show the way to the grave and must be brought together. Where the priests tell the stories still, the disc of the column may be found which will illuminate all and reveal the truth to him who brings the Tears to it. One Tear lost beyond the seas. One Tear carried by the pharaoh to a far away land. One Tear may only be found after the second one.

So, he had to find a disc that would light up when the Tears touched it. That made sense given how he'd seen the one interact with the wall in the Grand Canyon. Finding the disc could prove to be quite tricky. Still, the clue that was given was that it was where the priests still told the stories. His gut told him that was a reference to Egypt.

He looked at the clock and realized that it was nearly noon. He was beginning to get hungry, but even more than food he wanted sleep. It would still be early enough back in D.C. that he might be able to catch Dr. Reid at home.

He put the three Tears in his pocket and headed downstairs to the phone he'd seen in the lobby when he'd checked in earlier. He was able to get some change from the front desk and then he wedged himself into the small phone booth and began the process of placing his call.

When Dr. Reid finally answered he sagged in relief.

"Charles?" Dr. Reid asked.

"Yes, I'm fine."

"You...acquired what you were looking for?"

"Yes. I'm in Brussels now."

"That is a relief, I must admit."

"I've been up going over the tablet and the papers you gave me. I have to ask, who translated it?"

"A good man, but one lacking in imagination, I'm afraid."

"A great deal of imagination. I retranslated it."

"And what did you discover?"

"I think I'm going to end up in Egypt after all."

"How's that?"

"There's a reference to placing the Tears in their proper positions on a column that commemorates Atlantis."

“You’re thinking of the column that the priests of Neith in Sais showed to Solon?”

“Unless you’ve heard of another column somewhere in the world that talks about Atlantis.”

“I can’t say that I have.”

“Well, I know I haven’t, so that seems the best lead.”

“Godspeed, and if you need anything, please let me know what it is.”

“I will.”

Tex hung up. He hadn’t had the time to explain to Dr. Reid everything that had happened, including that Lena had saved him from capture by the Paris police. He was still puzzling that one over in his head. Was it professional courtesy or had she just figured it would be harder to steal the gemstones if they were in police custody?

He headed back to his room. He’d leave in the morning for Egypt. For now he needed to get some sleep and then he had some more research to do. Fortunately he had brought with him some of his books on Egyptology in case he needed them in translating the text of the tablet or understanding some of its context. He made it upstairs and fell quickly asleep.

When he awoke several hours later night had fallen. His stomach was now strenuously protesting the lack of food. He went downstairs and ate at the little restaurant there. When he was finished he made his way back upstairs to his room where he got out his Egyptology books and began to look things up. He had a few things he needed to review.

He believed that very little was currently left of what had once been the city of Sais in the Egyptian delta. He intended to find out as much as he could about the ancient temple there before traveling to the site and trying to figure out what to do from there. He quickly lost himself in the reading.

The goddess Neith was one of the earliest known Egyptian deities and the patron of Sais. She was a warrior goddess also associated with hunting who was frequently pictured with arrows. The Greeks considered her to be the same as their goddess Athena and so the kinship between Athens, the city of Athena, and Sais was felt by both places. In fact, Diodorus, a Greek historian, wrote that Athena built Sais before the great deluge that destroyed both Atlantis and Athens.

There was also a creator aspect to Neith as well, and she was associated with the primeval waters. She was called Mehetweret, the Great Flood.

Tex froze as that sense of being on the brink of discovery seized hold of him. If Neith was known as Mehetweret then it made sense that her city was the one that was devoted in ancient times to preservation of the story of Atlantis, an island consumed by water and sunk beneath the waves. In ancient times it would have made sense for the disc described in the tablet to reside in Sais.

Was it still there? There wasn't much left in that area anymore and what statues and stelae had been found were scattered around the world in various museums. If something had been transported to one of those muscums that spoke of the story of Atlantis he would have thought someone would have translated it and somewhere there would be rumors of its existence. Since there did not seem to be he had to assume that if the pillar still existed it had not yet been found.

He was seized by a sudden intense uneasiness. It was ridiculous. No one could possibly know he was here. He stood slowly and walked over to the window, looking down into the street. Something was wrong. He could feel it. He didn't know how he knew, he just did.

He turned quickly and packed everything he had back up. He glanced longingly at the bed which he'd hoped to spend more time in that night. That wasn't important now, though. What was important was keeping himself and the Tears safe.

He had to get to Egypt and quickly. He felt the urge pushing him, making him move faster and faster until it had propelled him to the door and down the stairs to the lobby then out to his waiting car. He didn't even bother checking out.

He started the car and drove quickly away from the hotel, sweat beginning to roll down his back. Something was wrong. He felt like there was an invisible clock ticking in his mind. Time was running out. Over and over one line from the tablet kept playing endlessly in his head, repeating itself until he thought he would go mad. It was about the windows of opportunity to restore Atlantis.

Once they close all is lost forever.

Chapter 19

Tex expected to feel better once he left Brussels behind. Instead he just continued to feel more anxiety bearing down on him. He had thought earlier to take a train to Egypt, but he realized that he had to limit his contact with people now until this was over. He couldn't risk delay of any sort. Plus he knew Lena was in Europe, and the woman had the most impressive habit of showing up where he least expected her.

He drove straight through the night, stopping at dawn by the side of the road to grab two hours sleep before pressing on. With every town he passed the drumbeat that told him time was running out grew louder in his head.

He stopped in smaller towns to get food and gas as he needed them and continued to take occasional naps on the side of the road. He was driven to see this through, to have an end to everything once and for all.

By the time he'd reached Athens he'd driven nearly two thousand miles. He couldn't help but reflect that it was appropriate that Athens, the sister city to Sais, and the city that figured prominently in the Atlantis stories, was his jumping off point in heading to Egypt.

In Athens he boarded a boat that took him across the Mediterranean Sea to Alexandria. From there he was able to rent a car. He drove for a few hours and finally reached Tanta after nightfall.

Even though the drumbeat was still pounding away in his head he knew that there was nothing he could do until morning so he checked into a hotel. He told the desk clerk that in the morning he would need a guide who could take him to Sais. The man agreed to procure him one and assured him that he would be able to leave in the morning. With that taken care of, Tex headed upstairs and fell asleep until morning.

Tex was up with the dawn. At breakfast the clerk from the night before approached him and told him that his guide would be picking him up outside the hotel in half an hour. Tex finished eating, grabbed his bags from his room, and headed downstairs.

Out front a man was waiting with two camels.

"You are looking to go to Sais?" he asked.

"Yes, you're the guide?" Tex asked.

"I am. Ammon is my name."

"Tex."

The man signaled the camels and they knelt. Ammon helped Tex secure his gear on his camel. Once that was done Tex mounted and the camel stood up. He had been on a camel before, but it always threw him how different their stride was to a horse.

As soon as his guide mounted his camel they turned the animals' heads toward the desert. At the edge of the city they paused to let the camels drink from troughs that were set up for that purpose.

"Always have a care for your camel," the guide said. "You take care of the animal, and it will take care of you."

"Sound advice," Tex said, waiting while the camel drank its fill. "How far is it?" Tex asked.

"About thirty kilometers. We will let our camels run for part of the way and we will be there inside two hours. Is this good?"

"Perfect," Tex said.

At last the animals were done drinking and they were on their way. The hot desert sand was hard to look at and Tex could feel the heat radiating off of it. He could feel himself already starting to dry out. Soon his lips would begin to crack from the lack of moisture in the air.

"You are an archaeologist?" his guide asked when they were well away from the city.

"Yes, I am."

"Usually archaeologists travel in groups. Some to dig, some to tell those where to dig. Some to study what was dug up."

"I'm not here on an official excavation. I'm just doing some research for a paper I'm writing."

"You are interested in Sais?"

"Yes."

"I could save you the trouble of the trip. There is nothing there anymore. The stones were taken centuries ago and used for other things. The mud brick walls farmers have been taking for a couple hundred years. They use them as fertilizer. There is very little left. It's hard to tell it was even once a city. You are the first archaeologist to care in a long time. What do you think you will find that others have not?"

The key to one of mankind's most enduring mysteries, he thought to himself. Out loud he said, "I don't know, something, maybe."

It was possible that he was on a wild goose chase and that the column he was seeking had been destroyed long ago. The more he listened to his guide the more he feared it might actually be true. He couldn't allow himself to become discouraged, though. He had come too far to give up at this point.

"What is it you're hoping to see, to find, that others have not?" his guide asked.

Using local guides was a necessity in his line of work. It always brought up a conundrum though. How much information did you share with them? In theory the more you shared the more they would be able to help you pinpoint what you were looking for. However, that could backfire. Sometimes knowing what you were looking for would make them increase the price you had to pay for their help. They could also realize that if one person was interested in something others might be and sell you out to a higher bidder. Or they could occasionally become protective of specific local artifacts or stories out of devotion, superstition, or just plain stubbornness.

"I'm looking for any remains of the temple complex, particularly anything with writing on it."

"Then I can save you the trouble, my friend. There is nothing like that left there."

"I just want to take a look for myself," Tex said.

"Okay, but it's a waste of time."

When they let the camels run it took a little bit for Tex to get used to the rhythm but he finally did. The animals could eat up a lot of ground really quickly, and many of their natural attributes made them ideally suited to travel in the desert.

He didn't know how long it was going to take him to find what he was looking for. He hoped that he would get lucky as he had in the Grand Canyon. While it was possible that he could find his way back to Tanta without his guide, he would not want to try. Being lost in the desert was far more dangerous than being lost on the Colorado River.

When they finally arrived at the location Tex could see what his guide had meant about everything being gone. There were only a handful of mud bricks left to show the location of what had likely once been a wall.

It was possible, if unlikely, that what he was looking for was covered over by the sand. Given the size that the temple was supposed to have been, though, it could take him weeks of digging just to figure out there was nothing to find.

He felt that scratching sensation again at the back of his mind. He didn't have weeks, he had to find it sooner than that. There had to be a way, he just needed to think.

He dismounted from his camel and walked slowly to the wall that was still partly standing. Aligning himself with it he turned and squinted. He could make out areas of discoloration, and an occasional lone brick. When he traced these all the way around with his eyes they formed a gigantic rectangle. This had to be the boundaries of the ancient temple. Somewhere in that space the column he needed to find had once resided. He just hoped it still did.

"What are you doing?" he heard his guide ask as he stepped forward, walking slowly into the space.

What he was doing was trying to imagine the layout in his mind based on other temples in the country that had been excavated and the ancient accounts of this one that he had read. He was trying to understand how the flow of people would have moved in and around it.

"Do you know if the entrance to the temple was facing this direction?" He asked, pointing to his right.

His guide didn't answer. The man probably didn't know.

Tex stepped forward again carefully, squinting as he tried to connect with what might have been there at one point in history.

"It is time to go," his guide said. "We need to get back before it is late, yes?"

Tex shook his head. "I'm going to be here for a while. There's something I must find."

"You will not be permitted."

Something in the man's tone sounded off.

"What does that mean?" Tex asked, turning quickly. As he turned something stung his arm. A moment later he heard the report of the gun that was suddenly in his guide's hand.

Chapter 20

Tex dropped to the ground as the man fired again. His hat went flying off his head. He yanked his own gun free and fired, hitting the man who tumbled off the camel and into the sand. Tex scrambled forward, yanking the gun away from the other man and tossing it. He had shot him in the chest and the man didn't have much time left.

"Why?" Tex asked.

"You can not be permitted," the man said, blood bubbling up on his lips.

"Who, who does not permit me?"

The man shook his head.

"Do you work with the others who carry the Helenium flower?" Tex asked.

It was too late, though, the man was gone.

With a shout of frustration Tex stood up. He was constantly being denied answers and it was making him crazy. Now he was going to be left to wonder if the dead man had friends that were going to be coming after him as well.

The stinging in his arm persisted and upon inspection he found that the bullet had just grazed it. He pulled some antiseptic and gauze from his satchel and bound it up as well as he could. Then he took a moment to gather himself before he bent down and searched the dead man.

When he found the card with the Helenium flower he wasn't surprised. Even though he hadn't been able to stop and confirm he was sure that the man who had attacked him in Paris as he was trying to make his getaway was also a member of this organization, whatever it was. He had been attacked almost immediately after finding each Tear, and now this man attacked him before he could look for the column and the disc that might make everything make sense.

Who were these men that they were willing to kill and die to stop him? Was their master after the secrets of Atlantis as well, setting men to attack him after he had accomplished each hurdle for him? If that was so, then why had this man not waited until he found the column and the disc? Either because he knew that Tex would not find them or because he was afraid that he would. Maybe they were trying to keep the secret.

It was all just speculation, wild theorizing at this point. At least the presence of the Helenium card on this man proved he wasn't crazy. These men, whoever they were and whatever their aims, were after him because he was trying to find Atlantis.

He stood up. Find Atlantis was exactly what he was going to do. He grabbed the small shovel that he had in his gear and walked back into the rectangle he had mapped out. He began to walk its perimeter slowly, eyes searching for anything, the slightest discoloration of sand even, that would tell him something about the place. It was slow going, the sand shifting beneath his feet. He had walked one length of the first wall and turned the corner when he had a sudden sense of déjà vu. He stopped walking. What he was doing was intensely similar to what he had done back in the great room in the cave system of the Grand Canyon. The walls there had been rock, but shaped and formed by tools.

The room had been massive, but smaller than this temple outline he was standing in. Unless you took into account the chambers like the pharaoh's burial chamber then it was probably roughly the same size.

After a minute's thought he oriented himself and headed for the wall here that faced the same direction as the wall in the cave should have. He walked to where he estimated about halfway down the wall would be. Then he began to traverse the area, walking back and forth starting next to the wall and moving slowly inward. He had made it several feet inside the perimeter when he felt the sand change under his feet. Suddenly it wasn't loose and shifting but it felt hard, as though it was being supported. He took a few more steps and the sensation reverted back to the looser feeling. He turned around and stepped back over the area where the sand had felt firmer.

It was possible there was something buried just below the surface. He slipped his bandana over his nose and mouth to keep the sand out. Then he took the shovel and began digging. Six inches down he struck something hard and he felt that flare of excitement again. He began pushing sand away from the area and slowly a stone shape began to emerge.

It was the top of a column. He began to dig faster, moving as much of the sand as he could and wishing he had a team of people to do this so that it wouldn't take so long. Slowly the sides of the column began to rise above the sand and he could see hieroglyphs on it.

His gut told him he had found the right column. Where would the disc be, though? He kept digging, fighting the urge to try and decipher each hieroglyph as it came into view. He'd have time when he was done hopefully to read it all.

The sun was broiling down and he forced himself to stop and get some water from his bags. He chafed at the delay but he knew from experience that it could be deadly to let the excitement of a discovery keep you from properly taking care of yourself in harsh climates.

He returned to work a few minutes later with renewed vigor. Little by little the column was emerging and he desperately wished he had a camera with him to capture it on film for Dr. Reid. If all went well, though, this very column might one day be enshrined in a new museum dedicated to Atlantean artifacts.

He had uncovered nearly three feet of it when he suddenly froze. He saw a tear-shaped indentation in the column. He ran his finger over it. The shape had become unmistakable to him.

He carefully removed one Tear from his pocket and pressed it into the indentation. The Tear began to heat quickly, turning red much faster than he'd ever seen it do before. There was a rumbling sound and he put his hand on the column. It felt as though the entire thing was vibrating. Around it the sand began to retreat more, revealing even more of the column. Then glowing finger marks appeared on the column as they had on the door to the burial chamber back in the Grand Canyon.

Tex pressed his fingers onto the spots and felt them actually give slightly beneath his touch. He was then able to slide a panel in the column to the side, like moving a pocket door. Behind it there was a small cavity with a metal disc that was about eight inches in diameter. He pulled it out and set it down on the sand to examine it. There, at its center, were three indentations, one for each Tear.

He retrieved the first Tear from the column. The panel remained open. He placed the Tear on the disc. Then he pulled the other two out of his pocket. His heart was in his throat as he placed the second one. Then, excitement and terror knifing through him, he placed the third Tear in its spot.

The Tears turned red hot, the entire disc began to glow, and then an image appeared in the air just above it. It was the face of a man. Tex stared at it in awe. It was like seeing a motion picture only there was no screen, the image just appeared in the air in front of him.

The mouth opened and strange words he didn't understand came out. It stopped speaking for a moment. Then it began to speak again. The language sounded different than the first that he had heard. It paused again. Then it restarted, spoke for a few seconds and then paused. When it started back up again the words sounded almost familiar, like Greek, but he couldn't follow. There was another pause. When the image began speaking again he recognized Latin.

Do you understand? the image asked.

Tex realized the image was somehow waiting for a response. "Ego agnosco," he replied, indicating clumsily that he understood.

The image nodded and then continued speaking slowly in Latin. Fortunately, it was going slowly enough that Tex could understand what it was saying.

You have this one chance to save Atlantis. Three times before it has been possible. Three times before it has remained lost. This is the last. Only weeks remain. You must seek out the Tears of Poseidon. The Tears of Man will help you find the city. The Tears of the god, Poseidon, will help you raise it from its grave.

"Where are the Tears of Poseidon?" Tex attempted to ask in Latin when the image paused.

It continued, although he wasn't sure if it had been meant to or if his question had spurred it on.

The first Tear of Poseidon lies in dust where once dwelt a woman of great beauty who inspired men to lust. Twice she was kidnapped. The first doomed a man, but the second doomed a city.

Helen of Troy. That was who the image was describing. Troy, which until a few decades before had been lost itself. This truly was the first chance someone would have had to restore Atlantis. And he owed that opportunity to a dreamer with a book.

The image winked out of existence. It hadn't told him anything about the location of the lost city except for the fact that the Tears he possessed should show its location. Before he could set off to figure out how to find it, though, he had three more orichalcum Tears to find.

He sat there for ten minutes, but nothing more happened. He slowly removed the Tears from the disc, securing them once more in his pocket. The disc he then carried to his satchel and carefully placed inside. He had a feeling he would need it later. Even if he didn't, though, it was at least something to show to Dr. Reid, proof of what it was he had found.

He turned back to the column and found he was easily able to slide the panel closed again. It moved into place with a click. He ran his hands down the column, admiring it. He should get his journal and at least copy down some of what was written there before he left this place.

He turned and walked back toward his camel and his bags. He put away his shovel and started to get out his journal. He turned and froze as he saw a dust cloud. Riders were coming. There were five of them on camels, and they were heading directly toward him. It was possible that their arrival had nothing to do with him, but he sincerely doubted that. He grabbed his gun and moved away from his camel. He stood there, gun held behind his back and waited for them to come to him.

A few minutes later they were slowing up their animals and then they came to a standstill before him. He noticed that while four of the riders were staring from him to the pillar the one on the far left was instead watching the other four. Those four began talking and gesturing excitedly amongst themselves.

Finally, one pushed his camel forward a step. "Who are you?"

"Tex Ravencroft, archaeologist and professor."

"You should not be here," the man said, glancing again at the pillar behind him. "You should not be seeing any of this."

"And why is that?" Tex asked.

"It is forbidden."

The man pulled a gun out of his robes. Tex shot him before he could take aim. As he turned his gun toward the others a report rang out. The rider on the left had shot the man he was next to. Tex registered that he must be on his side, or, at least, not on the side of the others. As the two on the far right reached for weapons Tex shot them both as well. They fell from their camels and lay still in the sand.

"Nice shooting, Tex," a voice from his past said.

He spun around, gun in hand, and stared as the last rider dismounted and stepped forward. Slender hands reached up to unwind the scarf that was covering all but the rider's hazel eyes. As it came free he stared in absolute shock at the ghost before him.

"Jeanette?" he whispered.

"How are you doing?" she asked him as she stepped toward him.

The hand that was holding his gun began to shake. She reached out and touched his hand, lowering it and the gun to his side. She smiled at him as she stood there, inches from him.

"You're dead. I killed you. I saw you die."

She reached up and put a hand on his cheek and it was warm and real and alive.

"I don't understand," he whispered.

"Not everything is what it seems to be," she said. She flicked her eyes behind him and then back to him. "But, I'm guessing you've finally figured that out."

Epilogue

Dr. Reid looked up from the manuscript he was reading as his cat jumped onto the table and made a chirping sound. A moment later a man dressed all in black came striding through the stacks. He had dark hair that had a touch of silver in it. He walked up and stretched out his hand to scratch the cat behind the ears and the little creature purred appreciatively.

"He's always liked you, Solomon," Dr. Reid said with a smile. "I must admit, I'm surprised you left your temple."

"Well, you only rarely leave your library, so I figured I'd visit you for a change, Nicodemus."

"It's Nicholas these days," Dr. Reid said.

Solomon shrugged. "How are things progressing?" he asked.

"Last I heard Charles was headed to Sais."

"Does he still have the tablet with him?"

"Yes, he retranslated it, too. When he comes back I will make sure that you get the tablet back."

"*If* he comes back. You know what kind of dangers are facing him."

"Some days I feel old," he admitted.

"You are old. We all are," Solomon said.

"Yes, but today I feel it. I have faith in Charles, though. If anyone can complete the tasks ahead it's him."

"He is quite remarkable from everything I've seen," Solomon said, drumming his fingers on the table. "Are you ever going to tell him the truth?"

Dr. Reid sighed. "I'm afraid he's had enough truth lately to last him a dozen lifetimes. I can't burden him with anything else."

Look for

THE BROTHERHOOD OF LIES

A Tex Ravencroft Adventure

Part II of the Atlantis Trilogy

Coming December 2014

ARCHAEOLOGY
IN
FICTION
BY
DR. SCOTT C. VIGUIÉ

Look for

ARCHAEOLOGY IN FICTION

Available Now

Popular fiction is filled with images of archaeologists as daring adventurers who constantly risk life and limb in the pursuit of fabulous antiquities of immense historical and monetary value. There are evil villains, great romances, and unknown perils lurking around every corner. That's the view many people have of archaeology. What is the truth, though, behind the myth and why have the myths persisted for so long? In this book you'll explore:

The fictions surrounding archaeology.

Why we as people love and perpetuate those fictions.

What the truth behind the fiction really is.

Sometimes truth really is stranger than fiction. Come along and explore both.

Made in the USA
Columbia, SC
03 July 2018